GRAVE REVELATIONS

THEODORE PYSH

Grave Revelations
Copyright © 2022 Theodore Pysh. All rights
reserved.

ISBN: 979-8-88796-488-1

Printed in the United States of America

"Happy Death Day!"

You are going to die! You just don't know when! You know your birthday and probably celebrate it every year. But the mystery is, when is your "Death Day?" Consider this: It could be today.

Surely, you're aware that each year you have been alive on this planet, you have unknowingly passed the date of your death without celebration or awareness. Perhaps you haven't passed it quite yet this year, or maybe you have, or, as I mentioned above, perhaps today's the day.

Not to worry, you have plenty of company. Everyone alive, or whoever lived, has gone through the same cycle.

The Father of our Country, George Washington, was born on February 22nd, 1732. He lived sixty-seven glorious years, and, for every single one of them, he went through the wind and cold and clouds of December 14th without fanfare, celebration, or fear, never experiencing the realization that it was the anniversary of his death.

William Shakespeare got a two for one. He entered this world and left it on the same date in April. For fifty-two years, he celebrated his birthday and unwittingly celebrated his death day simultaneously.

It is now 2045; you shouldn't be surprised to know that today, almost all vehicles are electric and autonomously driven. Digital currency like Bitcoin and others have replaced cash, checks, and credit cards. We've solved that pesky Global Warming problem with machines that mitigate carbon. Medical science has advanced to where a baby born today can expect to live one-hundred-twelve years.

But I digress. This book is about the most recent development regarding death dates: yours, mine, and everyone else's. It all started about 10 years ago with this Kerry Richmond fellow.

"Kerry Richmond"
(The numbers guy)

NUMBERS! REGARDLESS OF WHETHER YOU'RE a numbers person, the entire planet revolves around a series of digits arranged in a precise order. Think about it; your address, phone number, date of birth, social security number, license plate, VIN, credit/debit cards, numerous expiration dates, and an endless number of PINs and Passwords. Your entire life, your entire existence, is dependent on a series of numbers.

Kerry Richmond, a recent Cornell graduate (class of 2032) with a Ph.D. in Applied Mathematics and minors in both NextGen Software Development and Advanced Robotics, realized at a very young age that numbers 'make the world go round' and he intended to use that knowledge to build a meaningful and profitable career. Kerry was incredibly proud that he had achieved a 3.9 GPA during his four years at a prestigious Ivy League University. He was also full of himself. He carried his arrogance around with him like an appendage. This was brought on by the harassment he endured in High School. The athletes and popular boys would denigrate him because he was such a nerd. But, now with High School in the rear-view mirror, he was admired and venerated for his intelligence and deftness with real-world solutions to problems. His insecurities and half-doubting had morphed into an exceptionally good self-image and all the self-importance that accompanied it. He knew he was wonderful. What he didn't know, what he couldn't imagine, was that he would discover a mathematical 'key' that would eventually unlock a mystery that had both intrigued and eluded humanity since the beginning of time.

According to the 2032 edition of Wikipedia, **"An actuary is a business professional who deals with the measurement and management of risk and uncertainty."** As a Division Manager for United Global Life and Casualty, Mr. Kerry Richmond directed a workforce of 150 actuarial scientists tasked with designing mortality tables for their prospective clients, which will allow Global Life to competitively price their life insurance products to maximize profits. Kerry was in heaven; every issue that he dealt with was cut-and-dry, every solution was mathematically based, and he presided over a division that was 'predictably' profitable. Kerry had little patience with other individuals' imperfections and was known for having a 'short fuse' when one of his subordinates would make even the tiniest errors. Especially delicious was the fact that one of his old High School tormentors was now one of his employed. Kerry's turn! "Revenge is best served cold." His personality was completely devoid of empathy and ruled by numerical precision. Deviate from that precision in your work and he would chastise and debase you in front of the entire crew without regard for your humiliation. He was respected by his minions but chronically disliked.

The HR team at Global was constantly fielding complaints about his management style, but, despite his caustic demeanor, his division was astoundingly profitable for the company, and his tenure was secure. He knew numbers, how to extract and parse the data, and most importantly, how to analyze the resultant 'digital salad.' Analysis was THE key. Look for minor anomalies, minute variances, and crucial inconsistencies. He realized that if he could improve the efficiency of his division by even the smallest percentage, it would significantly impact Global's earnings and, by extension, his compensation.

Kerry had been with Global for two years, and he routinely brought his work home....

in a figurative sense. As a Division Manager, he was allowed remote access to all company records, including client life insurance applications extending as far back as 2012. This information was critical since it was imperative that he could utilize historical data to improve his team's mortality modeling. He spent untold hours 'tinkering' with vast amounts of data to wring the last ounce of predictability out of the actuarial process.

One Friday night, while enjoying his favorite adult beverage, he mused how incredible it would be if he could accurately predict the exact date that a person would die, a DEATH DAY. Every living human has a death day; they just don't know what it is. Oh well, he'd had a long day, he was tired, and he had a scheduled 8 AM tee time. His death day musings would have to wait for another time, he needed some sleep. Little did Kerry know that Friday, July 21, 2034, would go down in history as the day that the concept of Death Day was born!

His alarm went off like a klaxon in a firehouse; 6 AM rolled around, leaving Kerry feeling sleep-deprived. But he was anxious to get out on the golf course. Outside of his work, golf was his only passion, practically his lone physical activity, so he relished those days when he could get out and enjoy a round with the few friends who willingly endured his condescending manner. But it was not to be. An unexpected cold front had moved in overnight, and a surprise, heavy rain began to splatter on his windshield as he backed out of the garage. His first thought was one of frustration; how could all the sophisticated meteorological models have missed this storm? He wasn't amused. He watched the back end of his freshly washed vehicle being violated by the intense downpour. *"Damn it! Damn it!"* he pounded his fist on the dashboard. *"There goes the day!"* He pulled the now ½ clean car back into the garage.

As the garage door closed behind him and he came back inside the house, he first spotted that the computer in his office was still running; he forgot to turn it off when he went to bed. Since he never used the 'sleep' function, the screen was still brightly lit with only two words centered on a white page: **DEATH DAY**.

He had almost forgotten about his 'death day' musings the night before, but now on this dreary, stormy, morning with nothing to do for the rest of the day he decided that it couldn't hurt to attack this concept once more. Or die trying! (Pun intended). Where to begin?

Meanwhile, I'll bet this guy sleeps on a numbered pillowcase. Bet he was a fun prom date. But, watch what he does in the next chapter.

3

"Mystery Solved"

(The Miracle Worker)

KERRY HAD ALWAYS SUFFERED A LOVE/HATE relationship with the development of mortality tables for Global Life. He enjoyed the freedom that he was given to 'mine' the historical data from the company's files, he enjoyed the fact that his efforts led to increased accuracy leading to increased profits, and last, but certainly not least, he enjoyed a lifestyle that he never thought possible two short years ago. Nevertheless, Kerry increasingly began to focus, almost obsess, on death and although he knew it was not healthy there was nothing he could do; it was his job.

What would be the effect of knowing the exact date of your death? Kerry knew that this knowledge had moral, philosophical, religious, and even political consequences.

Fact: Everyone is going to die. Problem: How to accurately determine a person's EXACT date of death in advance. Solution/Methodology: Use historical data to build a predictive template that can be universally applied to the general population. Kerry thought to himself "sounds simple"; he knew that this project was anything but simple. A unique challenge that, if successful, would rewrite actuarial history.

It wasn't lost on Kerry that he was already involved in determining death dates for groups of people, the key here is the word groups. He and his team had always approached their mandate to create mortality tables by analyzing vast amounts of historical data from a group of individuals, aggregating the data, and re-applying the historical results to a specific set of prospective life insurance clients. If you were a lifelong smoker, used alcohol, had diabetes, and suffered from high blood pressure your policy would be 'rated' priced, 50% higher than a like-gendered, approximate aged, non-smoking, non-alcohol using, diabetes and high blood pressure-free individual. He deals with statistics on a group level based upon individual traits.

Okay, this narrows the challenge to a certain degree; what can he do to use the same set of data that he and his team have been using to create mortality tables for select groups of people and employ this same data to predict the EXACT date a person will die. He began parsing data in a different way than he had in the past. He believed that the correlation between a person's individual attributes and their death day was 'out there' somewhere. He envisioned his data washed across three roulette wheels: one with dates on the slots, the second with months on the slots, and a third with years on the slots. All the wheels were spinning at the same time and when they stopped that would be the death day. The amount of data that he would have to process would be enormous.

Kerry spent the balance of his Saturday just parsing data. He spent sixteen hours on Sunday developing an algorithm that would act as his roulette wheels. He called in sick on Monday so that he could create a second algorithm to analyze the results of his roulette wheel process. This should allow him to alter the composition of data fed into the wheels and see the results much quicker than if he tied to do it manually. By Tuesday morning he was ready to turn on his wheels of death. *"Here we go,"* he thought.

He had to go to work on Tuesday; the team needed his direction and input to complete several key projects that he was supposed to unveil at the August executive committee meeting. Once again, Kerry found himself snapping at his colleagues for petty reasons. This time, because he was anxious to find out how his algorithms were performing in his absence. He estimated that it could take up to ten hours to complete just one entire routine. Each routine contained different combinations of attributes across a database that contained millions of applicants. He realized, from a statistical standpoint, that it would be almost impossible to find the correct answer on his first run.

He couldn't stand it anymore. He fabricated a reason to leave work early and headed directly home. *"Thank God!"* His absence made his tongue-lashed minions beyond happy. Once there he suffered his first setback of Project Death Day. The 'wheels' algorithm had a bug in it. He immediately saw the problem and 'fixed' it, reset the routine, and, with impatient frustration, he began the process once again, from the beginning. This couldn't happen again, he had to come up with a workaround that would allow working on project 'Death Day' from his office. "OK!" He purchased another laptop for his office and configured it so that he could monitor his home PC from his office.

Three weeks later Kerry was getting discouraged. He had purchased two more PCs for his home so he could run several routines at once. He had already run over 150 different routines and hadn't even come close. *"Maybe this isn't even possible."*

He relied on Thomas Edison to keep him going. When his assistants became depressed with their inability to solve a problem, Edison exclaimed: "I have not failed, I have just found 10,000 ways that won't work". Kerry pressed on.

Kerry arose early one morning to check his project and to feed another set of data into his roulette wheels algorithm. He began to wonder how much longer he could keep this up. He didn't have a robust social life before, but now he could easily be mistaken for a cloistered monk. He loaded the new data into the computer, started the routine, and began to analyze the results of what he began to call the overnight 'churn'. He now had three computers running 24 hours per day and laughingly named them Mo, Larry, and Curley. Looking at Mo's results it was just more of the same, Larry provided him with just one more frustration, and Curley's results were different than anything he had seen prior to this.

The first person on the list, Karen, born August 3, 1917, deceased December 13, 1952, was highlighted and the word MATCH was next to her name. Kerry wrote the routine to highlight any entry that matched the roulette wheels algorithm's predictive death day and accompanied with the word MATCH in uppercase letters. He immediately logged into his work computer and double-checked Karen's date of birth and date of death; August 3, 1917, and December 13, 1952. He continued down the list, manually checking the results just to be sure. Lastly, he reviewed the one statistic that meant the most, Overall Predictive Accuracy (OPA). This metric indicated the percentage of death days that were predicted accurately by the Roulette Wheels Algorithm.

Kerry was astounded! The Overall Predictive Accuracy was measured at 98.6%. 98.6%! He had succeeded, it worked; he just sat in his home office speechless. He didn't know what to do next. He hadn't shared his death day concepts with anyone. He muttered to himself "what now?'. He hadn't given much thought to being successful; he hadn't even defined what success would be. Would it be an OPA of 33%, 50%, or even as much as 90%? He never dreamt that he could achieve an OPA of 98.6% but there it was. He would need to run a significant series of tests over the next week or maybe a month to prove the 98.6% OPA. THEN WHAT?

Well, by now, it looks like this guy is on his way to Bronze Statue territory.

4

Death Day:
The Reality

PROVING THE 98.6% OPA TURNED OUT to be easier than Kerry had originally thought. After he performed the required tests, the first person he contacted was an intellectual property attorney with an eye toward protecting himself as well as getting a legal opinion as to who owned the work product from the Death Day Project. Although he suspected from day one that Global Life may have a claim to his work product, he wanted to know where he stood from a legal standpoint.

His attorney's comments were not encouraging. Although Kerry was in possession of the source code, he had used company resources, specifically confidential historical data and to a lesser extent company time and equipment to complete his Project. His attorney explained quite succinctly what Kerry needed to do in order to bring Death Day to market; authorize his attorney to contact Global Life, lay out the facts and potential ramifications associated with the project, discuss possible 'next steps' and marketing opportunities, and attempt to reach an agreement that will maximize the potential profitability of the Death Day Project for all involved.

Kerry thought that this might be a more difficult chore than creating the algorithm in the first place. Kerry had read several horror stories regarding founders, inventors, and authors who had walked away from their creations with virtually nothing. Kerry Richmond vowed that this was not going to happen to him; if possible, he will make a deal with Global Life.

After several weeks of negotiation, an agreement was reached regarding the ownership and future of the Death Day Project. Going forward, Kerry would transfer the ownership of the Death Day source code to United Global Life and Casualty in exchange for a one-time payment of $25,000,000 to Kerry Richmond, an ongoing royalty of 15% of gross sales, and Global and Kerry would enter into a 10-year consulting agreement at $500,000 per year.

Both parties were generally pleased with the arrangement. Global would market and sell the Death Day product to consumers at a price no less than $3,500 per client prediction. Kerry would be available to assist the company with Death Day in any way they requested for up to 80 hours per month. The company would be responsible for all marketing and sales decisions and any/all attendant costs. Death Day had become a reality. But the term "Death Day" was too indelicate. Global Life would call it "The Prognosis Project." Kerry didn't care, *"Call it what you want, just write the check."*

Ten short years ago, in July of 2035, actuarial scientists at United Global Life and Casualty, collaborating with computers and Artificial Intelligence, have advanced so far that they now can accurately assess *the exact day, month, and year* an individual will experience their ending. They may also accurately assess the probable *cause* of their demise. Unless, of course, they die by their own hand or in a freak accident.

This scientific achievement has been clinically proven to be accurate within 98.6%, and the process is the proprietary, patented development of United Global Life and Casualty Company of Omaha, Nebraska. As you might imagine, it has been published and broadcast since the initial announcement was made. It's been streamed, texted, and discussed on every social media platform, Metaverse, and kitchen table in America Ad Nauseum!

Nobody wanted to talk about anything else! Once they knew the date and likely cause of their death, they were good to go if they avoided runaway beer trucks, avalanches, and suicidal depression.

But of course, the larger question is: "Do we *want* to know? If we garner this information, would we want to celebrate it the way we do our birthdays? *Should* we celebrate it? Or would knowing cause immeasurable stress? Would we sweat bullets every year the date comes around? Would we feel good the day after knowing we are still alive? Is it blasphemous? Have we compromised privileged information that belongs only to the realm of the Divine?"

So, things up here in 2045 get very interesting. if you're over the age of 25, and you can provide $3500 in digital currency (2045 monies), United Global Life and Casualty will be more than happy to sit you down for your life expectancy test. However, "Probable Cause" is an extra $750 option, so after $4250 in digital currency, citizens can emerge from the ordeal, knowing the exact date and way in which they will meet their maker.

Right now, you're probably thankful that you don't have to deal with this. Then again, you will probably be alive yourself when 2035 comes around. I mean, who knows? (Get it?)

Decisions, decisions! What to do? What to do? A few thousand bucks and some tests, and we see all, know all. Like the best piece of chocolate cake, you ever had, it's to die for!

5

"The Ugly Duckling"

THIS BRINGS US TO THE STORY OF Wesley Caulder. Wesley was a lifelong, fifty-four-year-old bachelor. This wasn't so much by choice as circumstance.

Many times, a homely child will grow into an elegant specimen of humanity. Unfortunately, this was not true in the case of Mr. Caulder. No need to go into specifics, except to say his physical attributes were...well, he just wasn't a 'looker.' To make matters worse, Wesley was almost completely devoid of social skills. And therefore, without the necessary tools to attract a mate, was never able to 'connect' with a person of the opposite sex.

It's been said that *"Life is a trade-off."* if you are denied one thing, you will acquire another. Evidence of this cliché was Wesley Caulder's IQ. It hovered somewhere around the Einstein area and provided him a mastery of the stock market and all things financial. In his solitude, Wesley Caulder became quite wealthy.

And, though money is *"The root of all evil,"* it can also be a powerful aphrodisiac! And so, into the life of Wesley Caulder came the 'Drop Dead Gorgeous' twenty-eight-year-old Sheila Burrket.   While it would be unfair to imply that the primary reason Ms. Sheila was with Wesley for his money; It would be unwise to ignore Mr. Caulder's twenty-six-year age differential and previous romantic track record to designate any other plausible explanation for her affection.

Not surprisingly, Wesley fell deeply in love with Sheila.   If not at 'first sight" certainly moments later. Few women had given him this kind of attention in his entire middle-aged life, and he intended to hold on to her no matter the cost, emotionally or financially.

He paid no attention, and frankly, didn't care about the possibility that Shelia had enjoined the relationship for his money.   Predictably, love being blind, it was just weeks into their communion after Wesley had showered her with all manner of gifts and money, that; bending down on one knee, he presented to her, the most dazzling, five-carat, D flawless, blue diamond ring, and asked for her hand in marriage.

Amazingly, (sarcasm there) tears welling in her eyes. Shelia accepted.

After a very expensive, and months-long, exotic honeymoon to the Maldives and the South Pacific, Shelia began to ponder just how long she would be married to Wesley. Wesley was too much in love to even think of suggesting a pre-nuptial before they married; and so, she would be entitled to at least one-half of Wesley's fortune. But, she thought, *"I wonder how much longer he'll live?"* If he met his end soon, she'd get the whole enchilada! And so...one day she decided to talk to her loving husband.

"Wes! Do you know what I think we should do? I think we should get that Global Life and Casualty assessment of just how long the two of us will live! What do you think baby?"

Wesley happily replied: *"Whatever you want sweetheart. I'm curious too. I figure I'm worth another twenty years or more, so let's do it!"*

And 'do it' they did.

$8500 in digital currency. Blood tests, DNA, RNA, Urine samples, medical history, family history, etc,. etc. and then, they just waited for the prognosis.

It didn't take long.

Unfortunately for Sheila, Wesley was expected to live another 32 years and she was destined to live another 56! His Death Day was ascertained to be February 12th, 2070, and hers, December 16th, 2094.

Sheila began thinking to herself: *"If I stay with him, I'll be sixty-six when he passes! Damn!"* The more she thought about it, the more concerned she became.

"Maybe it's just better to take one-half of his assets now and divorce him."

She decided to ask:

"Wesley Honey! Just how much money do we have?"

The question came out of nowhere. Wesley was perplexed by the unexpected inquiry.

"Uh, why do you want to know sweetheart? Do you need something?"

Sheila responded with a nervous quality to her voice: *"No no Baby! It's just if God forbid something happened to you, what would I do? Who would I call? I have no idea about our finances. Nothing!*

Well, love may be blind, but it's not deaf. Wesley was beginning to comprehend the 'Gold Digger' part of Sheila's romantic interest in him.

"Don't worry about it sweetheart, our estate attorney has it all taken care of."

With the suddenly obvious 'suspicious' look on Wesley's face, Sheila decided it would be imprudent to push the subject any further.

"Damn!"

But, alll's well that ends well. All of Sheila's consternation was for naught. One lovely summer evening, while Wesley was busy doing other things, Sheila decided to take an adventurous ride on the back of a motorcycle with a 'friend.' "(if you know what we mean). Neither Sheila nor her amorous friend bothered to abide by the law and put on a helmet but, at 146 mph. it wouldn't have made much difference. We wonder, dear reader if you have any idea what happens when you hit an unexpected dip in the road traveling at that wild, exhilarating speed just mentioned.

That's right. Things got ugly.

Upon hearing the news, Wesley Caulder was crestfallen. He had lost the love of his life. How could he bear to go on without her?

Well, he did.

6

"Re-Election"

IF YOU HAVEN'T THOUGHT ABOUT IT BY NOW, it's probably time we brought up another strategy some have tried to use to thwart the Global Life predictions for one's demise.

Some Individuals would pay for the information and if it came back that say, the cause of their death would be a heart attack, as was the case of our friend Robert, they would head off to the nearest cardiologist and get themselves treated for heart disease, thereby preventing the stated probable cause of death.

There are two problems with this strategic approach. First, Global stated the "probable" cause not the "certain" cause of death. Secondly, if the malady (whatever it was) were to rear its ugly head in the far future, there would be no signs of it or any way to treat it in the present.

If you don't show heart disease or pancreatic cancer or whatever right now, how can we treat it? Even today, we can edit DNA and such by using something called 'CRISPR'

(*Clustered Regularly Interspaced Short Palindromic Repeats*. Repetitive DNA sequences.) Whatever *that* means; It's still not a magic bullet. They (whomever *they* are) began developing it in 2007 and it's come a long way towards eliminating cancers and other terminal maladies. But still, many cancers and other life-threatening diseases aren't even discovered until it's too late.

So, as it turns out, life expectancy has expanded somewhat but we are all still mortal.

And, while it shouldn't be a surprise, this incredible United Global life and Casualty development has crept into politics. In our most recent election, incumbent President, fifty-one-year-old Corrine Sepulveda pulled a 'quickie' on her Republican opponent sixty-seven-year-old Janet Prohaska.

It would be naïve to believe that 'anyone' could become President of the United States without owing big favors to those who made it possible. Like it or not. Pick you favorite president, he or she will have been corrupted on the way to the altar. They will also have hundreds of legal (or illegal) ways to gather information on opponents.

In *every* election, the job of the campaign committee is to gather as much 'dirt' as possible on the opponent to dissuade the voting populace from casting a ballot for them.

Remember Richard Nixon and Watergate?

Anyway, it seems both Prez and candidate Prohaska had both signed up and paid the fee for the Global Life Prognosis Project.

With some commentary by a broadcast journalist, you may have heard politics called a 'Blood Sport' Most of us would agree that professional politicians (are there any other kind?) generally will do or say whatever it takes to get elected or re-elected.

In this instance, the United Global Life and Casualty prognosis program turned out to be the political 'Kiss of Death' for the challenger, Ms. Prohaska.

Anyway, it somehow leaked out (doesn't it always?) that according to the United Global death prognosis, Ms. Prohaska had a mere four and one-half years left to roam our planet and President Sepulveda was able to cheerfully announce that her report noted that *she* could look forward to another happy, prosperous, thirty-six-years. Of course, we were all astonished (sarcasm here), that taking a page out of 2016 President Donald Trump's playbook, President Sepulveda played Ms. Prochaska's handicap up for all it was worth.

Streaming political commercials came out everywhere with disparaging comments regarding challenging candidate Janet Prohaska. Ads like:

"Do you really want a president who's already known to be in poor health?"

And...

"Apparently, If elected, Ms. Prohaska won't even live long enough to serve a full term!

And...

"My opponent is a very sick individual"

(Some individuals, paying just 'casual' attention to the ads construed that to mean Ms. Prohaska was perverted.)

"I'm Corrine Sepulveda and I approve this message!"

(Shame on you, Corrine! What a thing to approve!)

After these demeaning campaign ads, Janet Prohaska was crestfallen. How could she counter?

I think we can all agree that that just wasn't very nice. And just how did Ms. Sepulveda find out about Ms. Prochaska's prognosis? Well, as they say: "Girls will be girls!" (Or something like that)

Now, it certainly wasn't illegal for our President, Ms. Sepulveda to cite the United Global 'Prognosis Project' results; how she acquired them is an entirely different matter. But certainly, it was at least unethical.

Looking down from his pedestal at United Global Life and Casualty, Kerry Richmond observed this situation with great consternation. For starters, he never liked Corrine Sepulveda. He didn't vote for her in the last election and wouldn't this time. For her to use *his* discovery to smear her opponent, just added insult to injury for him.

The Inaugural Ball was magnificent!

Guess who won.

7

"Stroke of Genius"

WELCOME BACK! I appreciate your continued interest. Things are really getting crazy up here in the future. Just to put your mind at ease, it turns out Einstein's theory of relativity is no longer just a theory. Now we call it "Einstein's Law." And though you've fast-forwarded to present-day 2045, you haven't aged even a second. It's all good.

Meanwhile, payments for 'Prognosis Project' test services are showing up faster than they can tabulate at the headquarters of United Global. Family fights are ensuing. Husbands, wives, girlfriends, boyfriends, bachelors, priests. and rabbis are tripping over themselves to pay the fee and acquire their personal bio. The information desk is swamped with inquiries!

Some people are asking: "Can I have my dog tested?" It's pure chaos at United Global Central. The company's stock has soared more than Six hundred percent! Speaking of that, don't bother looking to buy the stock back in your time. The company doesn't even exist in your world yet, and, up here, they went public just a few weeks before the announcement. Don't kill the messenger!

You may be wondering if Kerry Richmond had taken part in this circus. And, while it was tempting. He decided to stay on the sidelines for a while himself.

But we do know of a fellow who decided to game the system without paying. Permit us to introduce you to one, Robert Collier. Mr. Collier had known people who had paid the fee and were happily informed that they had decades left before they were likely to meet their maker. In addition, along with their bio report, many of them received an offer from United Global for term life insurance at literal rock bottom rates, as the company's own research showed them living far into the future.

Accordingly, the accuracy of the information was further validated, as he had heard of others who met their end on the very day and in the way it was predicted. And, while the bad news was not welcome, some were comforted by the fact that it allowed them to mend old grudges and grievances they would not have been able to do had they not had this information in hand before the grim reaper arrived.

So, what to do? Robert was ambivalent. But what if the news was good? Both of his parents had lived long lives. His mother was still alive at ninety-one and, his father survived to eighty-eight. Wasn't it likely he inherited those long-lived genes?

Still, four thousand- dollars (or Yuan). The Chinese Yuan is now the world's preferred reserve digital currency; that was a tidy sum to pay, and Robert didn't have that kind of money just lying around. But then he had what could arguably be called a "stroke of genius"

The company's name was United Global *Life* and Casualty! Life! The keyword! Robert thought *"Why not apply for life insurance with them? Of course!"* As we're sure you know, *when* you apply for life insurance, they don't just *give* it to you because you pay the premium. Before they issue a policy, there's a mandatory physical, paid for by the Insurance company. Blood is drawn, urine taken, family history, etc. Are you a smoker? (Though hardly anyone smokes anymore). Do drugs?

If the Insurance company declines your application, they are required by law to provide you with the reason for their declination, just as companies who issue a credit of one kind, or another are required to furnish you with the reason for rejection if your application is denied.

And so, our friend Robert (we always called him Bob) decided to submit his application for life insurance. He considered he was sure he was in near-perfect health, and, at forty-seven years old he felt he was probably late in acquiring insurance for his family anyway. After all, he was the breadwinner.

Robert M. Collier, Registered Financial Advisor, $340K a year. He recommended life insurance to virtually all his clients but had none of his own. *"You teach best what you need to learn!"* His wife was a stay-at-home mom, and the kids were almost college age. What if he died unexpectantly? What would they do? And so, it was a logical, prudent decision to apply as soon as possible.

Twenty-year-term, $1,000,000 digital dollars. Surely, they would approve his application and then, even though he still would not know the exact date of his passing, the insurance approval would demonstrate, in the absence of an accident, that his demise was at least twenty years in the future.

Robert contacted a Global Insurance agent and got the ball rolling. The agent was beyond happy to write the policy. One million dollars, forty-five-hundred-a -year, and term policies paid 90% commissions on the first-year premium. Robert felt some real peace of mind in purchasing this policy and, at the same time, he had circumvented the 'Prognosis Project' fee.

In the interim, literally, tens of thousands of people were happily paying their thousands upfront to secure the unlocked answer to the mystery of when and how their lives would end.

Two weeks went by, and an associate of Robert's came into the office with a big, satisfied smile on his face. He had just received his insurance prognosis. If they were right, he had forty-three more years of life to look forward to. He purchased a report for his wife as well and barring any unforeseen circumstance, she had another forty-seven! She didn't like the idea of being widowed even that far in the future but still, this was great news! After work, the drinks were on him.

Robert was happy for his friend, and a little jealous. He wondered when his insurance policy would arrive in the mail. (Yes, dear reader, even in 2045 we still have the post office and even mailboxes. Government agencies *never* go away!) He was sure he would be getting good news himself.

He arrived home around seven that evening, feeling a little tipsy from the celebration hosted by his ebullient co-worker.

He parked the car in the garage and half stumbled out to the mailbox. There it was. The Insurance policy. The envelope was not quite as thick as he thought it should be, but the return address was Global Life and Casualty. It had arrived in all its glory. Robert turned and half-ran toward the front door of the house eager to read the newly arrived mail. And then it happened. First, a feeling of doom came over him, followed quickly by the sharpest pain he had ever known slamming into his chest and throwing him to his knees on the snow-covered sidewalk.

He tried getting up, but it was like there was an anchor tied to his neck pulling him to the cement. He let out a feeble cry for help as he went back down; this time collapsing forward off his knees and spread-eagled into the snow. Consciousness now eluded him. The pain was gone, and his world was only blackness.

Hearing the commotion outside, Robert's wife opened the door and came outside to see her husband sprawled face down on the cement, the mail still clutched in his hand. She ran to him, turning him over and screaming his name. *"Bob! What's wrong! Bob! Please get up! Oh my God!"*

He was too heavy for her to lift. She quickly ran into the house and dialed 911. But it was not to be. Robert had suffered a massive aneurism and died that night, right there on the sidewalk in front of his home.

Almost a week had passed since Robert had died. With the funeral and all the commotion involved, Robert's wife hadn't thought to open the mail. Finally, in a moment of peace, she picked up the letter from United Global Life and Casualty. As she read the words it all seemed prophetic:

UNITED GLOBAL LIFE AND CASUALTY

November 19th, 2038

Dear Mr. Collier:

We appreciate your recent application for insurance with United Global Life and Casualty. However, we regret to inform you that we are unable to insure your life.

We are required by law to inform you of the reason(s) for our decision. Regarding this Matter, we regret to inform you that through your blood panel, urinalysis, DNA swab, and other diagnostic elements, we have discovered an advanced heart disease condition that places you in imminent danger of cardiac arrest, possibly resulting in death.

We urge you to consult your physician at your earliest opportunity in order to avoid a possible catastrophic physical event.

We thank you again for your interest in United Global Life and Casualty.

Sincerely,

John Holland,
Chief Underwriter,
United Global Life and Casualty

And so, as it turns out, Robert's "Stroke of Genius" was apparently a real stroke. He did avoid paying the 'Prognosis Project' fee, so he saved a few bucks there, but...when I heard about his passing, I could only consider the irony of it all. His poor wife! I should call her and offer condolences

8

"Rags to Riches"

SPEAKING OF MONEY, even if you're reading this in June, let us be the first to say: "Merry Christmas!"

Samantha Johnson was a young woman with a flawless, creamy complexion, eyes like liquid blue diamonds, a body to die for, and an engaging personality.

Growing up, Samantha was never hungry or cold. Still, she came from a very modest socio-economic upbringing. Mom and Dad never went to college. She too was denied that privilege.

However, though not formally educated, Samantha's father was not lacking in wisdom. One day, he uttered something that stuck with her: *"Baby, never marry for money. Hang around rich people, then marry for love!"*

And that is just what Ms. Johnson did. Soon after high school graduation, following her father's sage advice, Samantha scored a job waiting tables at the nearby Happy Hollow Country Club.

What better place to make her father's advice come to fruition? There were plenty of wealthy young men who regularly dined at the club with their parents.

Samantha was easy to look at. And, while her persona demonstrated that she was a superb female specimen, with high standards and mores; those qualities weren't necessary, as the testosterone factories that accompanied virtually all the aforementioned young men were all working double shifts.

One day, while she was serving dinner, young Charles Wister, of the Philadelphia Wister family, dragged up the courage to ask the young server if she might be interested in spending some time with him outside the confines of the club.

Charles himself was not an unattractive sort. Rather, he was a graduate of an IVY League university and worked for his father in their global software enterprise.

Samantha eagerly agreed. One evening out led to another and another and then another, and soon Charles and Samantha became an item. Eventually, Charles bent down on that proverbial one knee and proposed marriage.

Charles' parents were somewhat distressed by him marrying "below his station" but he cared not. On Samantha's side, the family was elated.

The wedding was an extravagant, eloquent affair, attended by all the local dignitaries and Samantha's father proudly walked her down the aisle in his just purchased Goodwill suit and 'clip-on' tie.

It was obvious by the looks on their faces that everyone in the Wister family was aghast at this display of lower socioeconomic attire. The ignominious (whatever that means) emotions they experienced having the world see their offspring willingly stoop to such vulgar marital social sophistication was nearly unbearable.

The reception dinner displayed even more indelicate social atrocities, as the Johnson family simply 'chowed down' unaware of dining etiquette or protocol. Samantha too was oblivious to any social infringements.

They say: *"Money can't buy happiness!"* and while that's been proven true time and again, no one seems to mention that it's also true that you can *'rent it'* for a very long time.

Several years later, it was beginning to look like the 'lease' on the happiness rental policy was coming to an end. As we stated earlier, even in the beginning, Charles' parents had some real consternation about their only child marrying a commoner. To make matters worse, almost five years later there were still no signs of a hoped-for grandchild.

To them, it was bad enough that Samantha was an uneducated peasant type who had no sense of protocol in their perceived high society circle of associates; surely that could have been mitigated by presenting them with an heir to the father's financial empire. But when even that was not forthcoming, the family began to unabashedly snub poor Samantha; conveniently forgetting to include her in the family get-togethers and holidays. It's often been said *"Familiarity breeds contempt!"* and so, Charles too was beginning to lose interest and resent his betrothed.

The cold-shouldered attitude of the Wister family was not lost on poor Samantha. Every day presented a new flavor of humiliation and snide remarks. Holidays were the worst. Those events ended with Samantha crying herself to sleep.

As one might expect, after five years of marriage, boredom had replaced fascination, and Charles was looking elsewhere for comfort and companionship. Easy to find when you have money. Charles was in the midst of an affair with another more, shall we say "appropriate" nubile associate.

Perhaps out of cowardice to ask for a divorce, and the accompanying appendage of guilt, Charles began to abuse Samantha. Not so much physically, though there were infrequent bouts of shoving and shouting, but with verbal attacks and a rapier tongue that sliced her already fragile self-image to shreds.

In a word, Samantha was 'miserable' and living in a 'cage with golden bars.' Her own thoughts of divorce would not stand in her Catholic upbringing. Samantha's parents would be mortified. Good Catholics don't get divorced. You find a way to make the marriage work. Besides, her parents weren't aware of the almost daily abuse and snobbery of Charles and his family.

She had heard or read somewhere about the United Global Casualty and Life 'Prognosis Project' that could accurately predict an individual's 'Death Day.'

Without Charles' knowledge, she sent off $3500 in digital coin to Global life. She wasn't interested in the probable cause of death so much as the date she could expect her demise.

Two weeks later, the prognosis came back. Samantha Johnson Wister would likely meet her end on Christmas day, December 25th, 2057. The probable cause of death would remain a mystery unless she forwarded yet another $750 in digital currency.

Samantha found this interesting. She looked up famous people who had died on Christmas Day and they included Charlie Chaplin, Dean Martin, Jon Benet Ramsey (murdered at 6 years old) a few obscure emperors and kings, and, a woman named Eartha Kitt, who ironically sang the famous pop Christmas classic "Santa Baby."

As expected, the report didn't state the "probable cause" of Samantha's demise, but the date was Christmas Day, 19 years forward.

She would still be a relatively young woman, but Samantha lacked the will and fortitude to endure this misery for an additional two decades.

On a scale of miserable from one to ten, Samantha was a twelve. She was depressed, despondent, unloved, and unwanted. Christmas 2039 was just a few weeks away.

She arranged with her therapist to prescribe a powerful sedative to counteract depression and purchased some maximum strength Tylenol and an expensive bottle of Opus One wine.

Christmas morning, 2039, she came downstairs and opened her gifts and cards, all sterile and devoid of loving emotion. After a Christmas morning celebratory brunch, Samantha retired to her opulent bedroom and ingested the entire bottle of sedatives and Tylenol, finishing off with as much of the wine as she could tolerate.

Ninety minutes later, Samantha passed on to what we all hope is a better place. As she lie there going in and out of consciousness, at first, she wondered if United Global Life and

Casualty would have predicted the probable cause of death as suicide. Unlikely.

And so, it was "Goodbye Charles and family. Goodbye Daddy and Mommy. Goodbye to the initially rented 'Monetary Happiness Lease.' Samantha had joined the exclusive club of the "Christmas Day Dead." And, at least United Global got the day right!

It did help to validate the statistical reporting that wealthy individuals are the most likely to commit suicide. The more wealth, the higher chances of death by your own hand.

Interesting huh?

9

"Doctor Knows Best"

Wɪᴛʜ ᴀʟʟ ᴛʜᴇ ᴄʜᴀᴏꜱ ᴀɴᴅ ᴄᴏɴꜱᴛᴇʀɴᴀᴛɪᴏɴ caused by this newly developed technology, it is no wonder Kerry Richmond has so far declined to experiment with it himself.

But, as we've seen, many people have taken the bait. How does the saying go? *"Curiosity killed the cat!"* Well, the cat's not all it killed. You pay your money you take your chances. Ok! It's *your* life. (Literally).

And so now comes the story of Ronny Osborne. Ronny wasn't rich, but he *was* a curious sort. Upon hearing of the new United Global Life and Casualty development, he eagerly cobbled together four-thousand-two-hundred-fifty dollars and scurried down to his local, hometown, Global Life offices and ordered the premium package. Date and year of his passing, probable cause of death, the whole program!

He willingly let them draw his blood, swab his saliva, peed in a cup, and filled out the ancestral background and lifestyle questionnaire.

The manager of the local office told Ronny that, because of the extreme demand for the product, there would be a short delay in getting the results back to him. It would take maybe three or four weeks. And when the results came back to the local office, they would notify him by whichever means he preferred.

With that, Ronny Osborne handed over the money and received an electronic receipt. He was not a patient man, but in this instance, he had no real choice. There was only one company with the technology to assess and prognosticate his future or, perhaps his lack of one.

The next three weeks went by very slowly for Mr. Osborne. He was filled with anticipatory anxiety. Waiting. Waiting. Until two- and-one-half weeks after his visit, he was notified that his sealed result package had arrived at the local Global offices.

They also reminded him that the offices closed promptly at three p.m. and since it was almost three now, could he just wait until tomorrow?

"No! No! I'm just minutes away! I'll be right down! Please don't lock up until I get there!"

The woman on the phone (yes, we still talk on sophisticated phone-like devices up here in the future Though, they're mostly micro-chips embedded under our skin.)

Anyway, enough of that. The fact is that forty-one-year-old, Ronald W. Osborne made it before closing and retrieved his sealed actuarial results.

He couldn't wait. Standing outside, just as the office door closed behind him, he ripped oper the envelope and read the assessment right there on the sidewalk.

It wasn't good.

The documents expressed sincere regret that Mr. Osborne was likely to die of a massive stroke, on April 23rd, 2039. Just a few months from now.

This wasn't at all what he expected. What kind of a report was this? He experienced an immediate, mild panic attack, ran to his vehicle, and immediately called his cardiologist. He needed an appointment like *"Right now!"* Surely, his cardiologist could run a battery of tests and discover what the problem was with his circulatory system.

It was a cool November afternoon, but Ronny was perspiring profusely. Phone's ringing and ringing and ringing and no answer.

"Christ! Somebody answer the phone! I'm going to die!"

Finally: *"Hello! Doctor Sojka's office how can I help you?"*

Ronny: *Hello! Look! I'm dying here! I need to see Doctor Sojka right away!"*

Astonished, the clerk asked: *"Excuse me sir. Did you say you're dying?"*

"Yes! I'm dying! I need to see Doctor Sojka immediately!"

"Well sir, that's quite impossible but, if you're dying perhaps, you should get yourself to the hospital."

"Ok, I'm not dying right this minute, but I'm going to die soon. I need to see the doctor as soon as possible."

The clerk responded: *"I understand.* (Though he really didn't) *I have an opening tomorrow morning at 7:30 or 9:30 a.m. Which would you prefer?"*

"7:30 tomorrow! Don't you have anything sooner?"

"No sir, the clinic doesn't open until 7 a.m. Would you prefer a tele-med visit this evening with one of our interns?"

Again, this time in obvious panic:

"No! No! **Hell No!** *I'll just take the 7:30!"*

"That's fine sir! Doctor Sojka will see you tomorrow at 7:30"

With that, Ronny swept his hand over the talkie chip in his arm and did the 2038 version of hanging up. Wiping the perspiration from his brow, He thought to himself:

"Maybe he can prescribe one of the new drugs or procedures they must have to prevent such

a thing from happening and there-by avoid this horrific prognosis."

This was impossibly hard. Maybe he shouldn't have paid to have this thing done. But, then again, what if he hadn't? He would have just dropped dead next April 23rd without warning. No, it was good he found out. Now, he could do something about it.

Not surprisingly, Ronny showed up at 7 a.m. the next morning, just as they were opening the doors. He was the doctor's first appointment of the day, and the wait was very short.

"So. Mr. Osborne. It's good to see you! How are you feeling these days?"

"I feel 'ok' Doctor Sojka, but apparently, I'm not."

"Oh? What seems to be the problem?"

With that, Ronny Osborne explained the entire ordeal regarding United Global Life and Casualty and asked the Doctor to test and treat him so he could prevent his predicted April demise.

After listening to Ronny, the Doctor expressed a disparaging opinion about this new development from United Global. He'd heard about it and was unimpressed. He told Ronny Osborne that he'd accommodate him and run some tests but, he was quite sure it was a false alarm.

And so, the battery of tests began. Stress tests, nuclear tests, Cat Scans, and all the other latest technologies developed to discover anomalies in the heart and circulatory system.

Ronald Osborne passed, as they say, *"with flying colors."* Just as his cardiologist suspected, they could find nothing abnormal about his cardio condition.   Apparently, Mr. Ronald W. Osborne had just wasted $4250 in digital cash. Not to mention the accompanying anxiety that came with it.

Still, he was nervous.   As April 23rd, 2039, drew closer, he became more and more anxious.

"What if my doctor was wrong and they were right? Surely that's possible!"

Finally, it arrived.   It was a Saturday and, even with his prescribed sedative, Ronald W. Osborne was not able to sleep the night before. That morning, he got up out of bed, showered, shaved, and drove to the nearest hospital emergency room. Though he felt fine, he walked in complaining of chest pains and shortness of breath.   He wanted to be near health professionals, just in case the insurance company was more accurate than his cardiologist.

Though his blood pressure was perfectly normal and blood tests indicated no signs of cardiac trouble, he insisted he be admitted to the hospital. And so, it went.

Saturday, April 23, 2039, was the longest day of Ronny Osborne's life.   He pushed the call

button on his hospital bed every 20 minutes.
The shift nurse would come in and ask what
the problem was, and he'd ask if she would
check his blood pressure and pulse.

The nurse calmly explained that if he had
a blood pressure issue the machine where he
was hooked up would send bells ringing and
alerts would buzz at the nurse's station. Very
tired from lack of sleep the night before, his
body finally demanded he fall to sleep and he
was awakened at 7 a.m. the next morning
Sunday, April 24th, 2039 by his cardiologist,
Doctor Sojka standing over him with a disgusted
look on his face.

He spoke to Ronny in a condescending voice.

*"Well, Mr. Osborne, I see you didn't pass on to
the unearthly world of the Divine last night"*

Sheepishly looking back up at him Ronny
retorted in a voice, half embarrassed, half
relieved:

"No sir. I guess not."

*"Ok Ronald let's get you up and out of this bed
and stop all the nonsense. Time for you to go home."*

*"Yes sir! I guess that's a good idea. I'm so sorry
for causing all this trouble."*

We really couldn't blame Ronny Osborne for
his paranoid actions. Really, what would any of
us do finding ourselves in the same situation?
And, on the drive home, he was reminded that

United Global *did* say their actuarial predictions were only accurate to within 98.6%.

His cardiologist suggested he file a class action lawsuit against United Global on behalf of himself and all the hundreds of other individuals who had succumbed to United Global's marketing claims. However, Ronald W. Osborne was simply relieved.

If he was aware of Mr. Osborne's situation, our developer Kerry Richmond would have taken great interest in a case study. And, if there *was* a lawsuit, maybe he would.

Ronny was out $4250 in digital but, at least he was on the right side of the grass. However, ten days later, what happened was inexplicable. While driving to his girlfriend's house to pick her up for their celebratory anniversary dinner, a horrific, unbearably sharp, head-pounding pain struck him right in his forehead, rendering him immediately unconscious. These days cars pretty much drive themselves without human intervention, so the car just kept going with Ronny's head lying on the steering wheel causing the horn to blast incessantly as other vehicles passed, the passengers looking on in disbelief. Eventually, it just slowed to a stop.

It's true, United Global Life and Casualty was wrong. (Sort of) But only by 10 days. That accounts for the stated, 98.6% accuracy.

Upon hearing the news of Ronny's passing, his cardiologist was incredulous. Chalk one up for Kerry Richmond and good ole' United Global Life and Casualty.

Better late than never!

10

"A Star is Bored"

Poor Ronny huh? Everybody, even his cardiologist, told him he was just paranoid, and the 'Death Day' purchase was all hocus pocus and smoke and mirrors and a big waste of money. And, when he's finally persuaded it was all just a big scam... Sayonara Mr. Osborne!

Well, what can *we* do? Wanna go to the movies? It probably doesn't sound like such a good idea to you back there in the 2020s. After all, not too long ago, you went through that Covid 19 pandemic thing. We understand, the movie industry, and especially the movie *theatre* industry was hit hard. Even before that Covid19 pandemic, the movie theatre industry was waning. The pandemic pushed the 'Screw you button' on the theatre industry's financial elevator and it quickly dropped down to the bottom floor.

Anyway, it's different now. When television came to American households in the 1940s, everyone thought movie theatres would go the way of the buggy whip. But theatres reinvented themselves and did just fine. Then, your big-screen TVs came along at the turn of the century; some home TVs were almost as large as actual movie theatre screens. Still, they survived.

Now, in 2040 (you're gonna love this) movies come packaged in holograms. All the theatres have been renovated into 'Theatre in the Round' The theatre projects a hologram down to the center of the room, and if you have a front-row seat, (which costs more) it's like the actors and action are right there in front of you in 3D.

But you may be asking why we brought all this up. Well, it seems a very well-known contemporary actor named Jamon Coronado, had a bizarre and morbid sense of dark humor. He's the 2040 version of Brad Pitt. Anyway, not knowing what else to do with his money, he purchased the United Global 'Death Day' report for himself. Long story short, according to United Global, he didn't have much more time left on the planet.

It's been said: *"Everybody wants to go to heaven; nobody wants to die."*

But that phrase did not apply to the perverse Mr. Coronado. He loved the idea of the 'last great adventure' of breathing his final breath.

Soooo.... he decided to have a "Death Day" celebration the day before he was supposed to depart the worldly chains of Planet Earth. He invited a slew of individuals: Childhood friends, enemies, ex-wives, (the same thing, really) associates, other celebrities, politicians, chauffeurs, bodyguards, etc. Literally, hundreds of people were invited to his 'Day before his Death Day Farewell Party.' And encouraged to bring sympathy cards. United Global had reckoned his 'Death Day' to be Saturday, November 20, 2038. And so, Friday the 19th was a perfect weekend lead-in! His mansion was decorated with perfunctory black balloons and blow-up Halloween-type headstones. There were T-shirts for all guests with a big "Joseph Coronado RIP" printed on the front.

But there was one little fly in the ointment: Mr. Coronado never purchased the 'probable cause of death' option from United Global. He preferred to keep it a mystery, even to himself. And, a week before his party, he felt absolutely magnificent. Didn't matter. Jamon Coronado was known to be a little, shall we say, 'odd.' He found this situation to be perversely intriguing. He liked his death being scheduled (sort of) without the melancholy burden of suicide.

"What if I die during my party? What fun! What if I don't die at all? Anyway, it needs to be quick. And I imagine it will be, given that I feel terrific. Beyond terrific really. I wonder what's wrong?

I'll bet I'm going to die of boredom. Can you die of boredom? OR maybe I'll die laughing at some lame joke someone tells. Can you prognosticate (big word huh?) someone dying of laughter? Well, we'll see! It's going to be interesting to see who shows up at my party."

He did take the time to write out his will. Jamon had no children. But, even if he did, he'd relish the joke that he left everything to his pet pot-bellied pig named Roscoe. Roscoe would live out his years in luxury.

As it turned out, almost a hundred souls showed. Admittedly, most were there out of curiosity more than anything. Everybody stops to watch a train wreck and, if you'll excuse the metaphor, that's exactly what this was.

It was a grand 'off the rails' affair! And weird. Many of the partygoers weren't sure of the correct protocol. How do you express your sympathy to the guy who's going to die, but isn't dead yet? *"I'm sorry for your loss?"* Is he losing himself?

Jamon Coronado reveled in the morbid attention. The paparazzi were there. All of the social periodicals were in attendance. The party started at 7 p.m. and went on into the next morning. Hologram Movie Star Jamon Coronado stayed awake for every thrilling moment. And, as the clock struck midnight on November 20th, 2038. He still felt fine.

"Maybe it'll happen later in the day today. I'm drunk and hyped up with cocaine but, I feel pretty good. Damn good really!"

There was a reason for that. Jamon Coronado didn't die on November 20th, 2038. In fact, he just finished a new movie almost two years after he was supposed to take the big dump.

Should he ask United Global for a refund? After all, they were 'Dead Wrong!' (pun intended). Not gonna happen Jamon! Do you think the attorneys over at United Global didn't have air-tight disclaimers when things didn't go as planned? Read your contract.

But admittedly, the world was stunned. Not just because he didn't die as scheduled, but because he was so disappointed it didn't happen.

And so, nothing in this world being perfect. That onerous 98.6% accuracy wasn't just off. It was waaay off! United Global's public relations team had to do some serious damage control, given it was an A-List celebrity who felt he got duped. The party got international attention and so did Mr. Coronado's survival.

In case you're wondering, yes, Jamon Coronado was plenty pissed off. He called into United Global HQ and demanded to speak to the now-famous Kerry Richmond.

Almost no one in all of United Global liked Mr. Richmond, and maybe, especially the young woman working the front desk. He always grumbled back at her when she greeted him. She was more than happy to put the obviously irate Mr. Coronado through to that "A_ _hole. " (This should be fun.)

"Hello?"

"Hello, is this the illustrious Kerry Richmond, developer of the Prognosis Project?"

Kerry was at first very happy to receive the call. It sounded like maybe it was a fan.

'Why, yes, it is. How can I help you?"

"Let me tell you how you son-of-a-bitch!"

Now taken aback, Kerry panted, "What?"

"The is Jamon Coronado. THE Jamon Coronado! You told me I was gonna die and I didn't die! It's been months now and I STILL haven't died! I was all excited! I had a big gala event and now this! You owe me big you scammer!"

In his life, no one had ever talked like this to Kerry Richmond. He didn't know how to respond. He began to stammer.

"Well...well"

"I demand you tell me right here, right now when I'm going to die, or you'll be hearing from my attorney!"

Kerry thought: "is this guy nuts?" ("Well, Duh Kerry! Ya think?")

Kerry couldn't take it anymore; he pushed the hang-up button embedded in his forearm phone and fell back into his chair letting out a big belly full of breath. *"Whew!"*

After that, he never heard from Jamon Coronado again, but both he and United Global DID hear from Mr. Coronado's attorney.

The powers that be at United Global requested a conference with Kerry Richmond. Kerry willingly acquiesced.

Sitting at the big, long, mahogany conference table with the CEO of Global life at the head and all the officers seated down the sides, CEO Jonathan Perkins, began the conference nervously by asking the questions of Kerry, seated twelve feet away at the other end of the table.

"Mr. Richmond. Are you aware of an individual named Jamon Coronado?"

In an almost condescendingly manner, Mr. Richmond replied:

"Yes, Mr. Perkins, I know full well who his is."

Obviously offended by Kerry Richmond's tone, the irritated Jonathan Perkins asked:

"And are you aware that he is suing United Global Life and Casualty for 15 million dollars"

With a subtle snicker, Kerry answered apathetically:

"Yes, he's angry because he didn't die when we said he would. He actually called me and demanded that I immediately tell him when he was going to die. What a joke!"

The entire table of executives were now staring harshly at Kerry Richmond. The CEO was not amused.

Kerry Richmond wasn't intimidated by this display of consternation. He knew he was personally responsible for billions of profits for Global Life and Casualty. And his multi-million-dollar contract with the company was signed, sealed, and delivered. Not to be rescinded.

And so, with a mouthful of arrogance and sarcasm, Kerry Richmond confidently replied:

"Our contract disclaimer states a 98.6% accuracy success. In my opinion, Mr. Coronado is one certifiably crazy individual. He's angry because he didn't die. My algorithm is very very good, but it's not perfect. I'll remind you: 'The last perfect guy was crucified'! Let him sue. You'll prevail. "

Saying no more, Kerry Richmond then rose from his seat and silently walked out of the conference room

CEO Jonathan Perkins was speechless. With his whipping boy gone from the room, like it or not, the meeting was over.

Anyway, he was right. United Global Life and Casualty prevailed in court, and it all worked out in the end. But not Jamon Coronado's end. He's still around. Poor little Roscoe the potbellied pig? Well, he died. Now, he's in Hog Heaven.

11

"Motherly Love"

Isn't this something? All this chaos! I'll bet it makes you think twice about living out here to 2045. Well, there's no sense in our speculating about your thoughts.

Since you're still with me, I'll try to entertain you with another story related to those wonderful underwriters at United Global Life and Casualty.

Her name was Laura Culpepper. Laura was the youngest of five children of the illustrious Mr. & Mrs. Randall Culpepper, Esquire. Quite the adventurer, Mr. Culpepper came to his ending on a big game hunting expedition in South Africa. The lion was the one who was supposed to be destined for taxidermy but, that's not how the safari turned out. As far as we know, the lion is still romping around the Serengeti chasing his dinner. But sadly, Randall Culpepper will hunt no more.

As one might expect, Mr. Culpepper's safari guide was beside himself with grief and regret that he wasn't able to save Mr. Culpepper from the big cat's clutches, and he expressed his deepest sympathies in his letter to the widowed Mrs. in Aurora, Colorado.

To put it in a less than formal context, basically, the gist of the letter was: "Shit Happens!"

And so, Mrs. Culpepper was saddled with five children and no spouse to support her financially or emotionally. Fortunately, her oldest son was almost through college and his brother was going to graduate from high school in the fall. That left Laura and her two older sisters the only ones requiring 'full-time' motherhood.

Things weren't ideal in the Culpepper household, but there was some insurance money and they all got by without the shame and embarrassment of being homeless and poverty-stricken.

It wasn't long before Laura's two older sisters went the way of their elder brothers and moved on and out of the house, leaving just Laura and her mother to themselves.

Laura was now eighteen years old and destined to graduate high school in the Spring. Being Valedictorian of her class, and a National Merit Scholarship winner, Laura received 'full ride' scholarship offers from all the best Ivy League schools.

But there was one, serious problem. Blame it on stress, or any number of other stimuli, Laura's mother fell victim to a debilitating disease. She was unable to speak, dress, or even feed herself. You'd think, with all the technological advances in medical science they'd be able to diagnose just what was wrong with Mrs. Culpepper. Still, her malady remained a mystery.

They had some money. But, not near enough to put mom in a nursing home. and all of Laura's siblings had moved on and away and started families, and they all claimed there was no way any of them could take their mom in or care for her in any way. Laura would have to do it! And so, full-time caregiver Ms. Laura Culpepper would not be going to any IVY League University, meeting the man of her dreams, or starting a family. No career, no movies, no parties, no socializing, no going out anywhere except to shop for groceries, with mom in tow.

Eighteen-year-old high school graduate Laura Culpepper would not be going anywhere, anytime soon. She remembered her mom's mom had a similar mysterious health condition, and she still lived to be ninety-two!

The quick math meant that she would be fifty-something when her mother passed. The Valedictorian of Mount Pleasant High School could now look forward to a career as a full-time caregiver.

Laura sank into a deep depression. Her brothers and sisters had all but abandoned her and her mom and left her in this chasm of grief. Laura resented her self-interested brothers and sisters for this world they had relegated to her without concern for her own life opportunities. All the potential success and happiness ahead of her were now obstructed by sibling apathy. The extent of their communication was an occasional phone call and a card on Mother's Day.

"Desperate people do desperate things!"

And so, our girl devised an escape plan.

She had been in this living hell of a full-time caregiver for two-and-a-half years now. Seldom able to venture out into the world without mom in tow. Constantly cleaning up her mom's incontinent messes. Dressing her, bathing her, etc. And sadly, for Laura, life was devoid of any outside social connections. Tomorrow, she would contact United Global Life and Casualty and purchase a million-dollar, ten-year term, Life insurance policy, with her mother as beneficiary.

At twenty years old, she was sure she was in perfect health and, at her age, the premiums on the insurance policy would be very nominal.

It all went smoothly. United Global issued her the policy and the annual premiums were very small by today's standards.

For the next year and a half, Laura went about her business, dutifully taking care of her mother. She fed her, coddled her, set her outside in the sun; all the things a loving daughter should do. As her mom's 'power of attorney' she constructed a will that said, in the event of her death, mother would be placed in the most upscale nursing facility in the area.

Now, she would have 'peace of mind' knowing that if something should happen to her, there would be enough insurance money to put mom in a quality nursing home for the rest of her days. As mom was also acquiring a mild case of dementia, mercifully, she probably wouldn't even be aware she'd be moved.

That night, May 26[th,] 2035, Laura tucked her mom into bed. Afterward, she went downstairs and opened the front door wide. Subsequently, she climbed the stairs to her own bedroom. There, she placed her will and insurance policy neatly on her bedspread and turned on the fire alarm. Then, walking calmly into the bathroom Laura opened the medicine cabinet and pulled out a fine, new razor blade. She filled her bathroom tub up almost to the brim and lowered herself slowly into the warm, comforting water.

With that, she picked up the razor and, she cut the veins on both her right and left wrists vertically, just as the instructions said to do on the suicide website.

Soon, the fire department arrived, responding to the alarm Laura had set. seeing the front door wide open, they rushed inside looking for the fire that never was. Upon further investigation of the house, they discovered Mrs. Culpepper sound asleep in her bed.

And, of course, lying dead in the adjacent bedroom bathtub was Ms. Laura Culpepper. Apparently, she was thoughtful and courteous enough to make the suicidal mess in the bath, so clean-up would be easy for whoever was assigned the undesirable task.

Subsequently, one of the rescue squad woke Laura's mom and brought her to the hospital for observation. Except for her medical condition, she was just fine.

The next day, as Laura had stipulated in the will, mom was taken to the Good Samaritan extended care facility. The finest nursing facility in all of Colorado. Paid for by the insurance policy from United Global Life and Casualty.

Now, dear reader, you may say *"Wait! Laura Culpepper committed suicide! Insurance companies won't pay if the insured commits suicide!"*

And if that's your thinking, I'm here to tell you you're wrong. Literally, all life insurance policies come with something called a 'Suicide-Exclusion.'

What this means is, that the insurance company is not required by law to pay a beneficiary in the event of an insured suicide. However! *If an insured commits suicide after a life policy has been issued for two years or more, by law, the insurance company must pay the beneficiary.* And in *some* states (Colorado being one of them) the waiting period is just one year! Laura was an educated young woman. She knew the rules. It's a fact that 96% of life insurance policies are never paid out. But this one did, whether United Global liked it or not.

Obviously, with stories like Laura Culpepper's you can see it's not all rainbows and unicorns for our friends at United Global. Plus, they have some very unhealthy people whom they insured years ago before Kerry Richmond developed the 'Death Day' actuarial. In addition, Litigation of every size, color, and shape has ensued. Disgruntled people who didn't die when they said they would (like Jamon Coronado) and still haven't. Imagine the stress caused by their inaccuracy. And then there are the suits from competing insurance companies, challenging the patent rights to United Global's 'Death Day' Prognosis Project.

Now, the entire life insurance landscape has changed. While you still must go through an arduous process of testing and documentation to acquire life insurance, it's somewhat easier to get insurance from other, competing insurance companies who don't have the 'Death Day' technology to predict your last day on the planet.

Without your paying the fee, United Global won't reveal your 'Death Day' to you, but their underwriters will certainly use their proprietary actuarial technology in deciding whether to insure your life.

And, if United Global denies you insurance, don't even bother applying somewhere else. They'll ask if you've ever been denied insurance and if you were, even if all your tests come back perfect, they'll know that United Global knows something about you that makes you uninsurable to them.

As they say: *"A rising tide lifts all ships!"* The general public has caught on to this United Global dilemma, and so, for the most part, they go first to some other competing life insurance company. This has made for a 'booming' life insurance business for competitors. They've been able to raise life insurance rates by more than twenty percent. United Global has made it a seller's market, and the extra twenty percent bump in rate helps competitors to mitigate the risks of them insuring someone whom United Global wouldn't.

Still, though your chances of being denied insurance with United Global; if they do insure you, their rates are going to be considerably lower than almost any competitor, because they're pretty damn sure you're not going anywhere until after your policy expires. Plus, you'll have a good idea that your 'Death Day' must be far in the future. It's the same old trick that Mr. Collier tried to pull in the first chapter. Maybe it'll work this time! Just remember, they didn't construct those big, brick-and-mortar insurance buildings by paying claims.

Wanna Play?

"Double Your Pressure!"

THERE YOU ARE! I considered you might have set the book down after that last chapter. Anyway, I'm glad you're back. In this chapter, I'd like to tell you about two individuals named Donny and Ronny Vorhees. They're twins. In fact, they're *identical* twins! (See where this is going?)

Who could possibly be more interested in what their death day would be than two identical brothers born just two minutes apart? Would their death day be the same? Different? If different, by how much? They were both 35 when they applied for the answer to the mystery.

In fact, you'd think United Global would have paid *them* just to see the answer!

Didn't matter. Donny and Ronny were beyond curious to find out; and so, they paid the $3500 digital plus the extra $750 'probable cause' option and waited for the results.

Six weeks went by, and still, there was no answer. As we expressed earlier, United

Global has been swamped with 'Death Day' applications. There's been a big, bottlenecked backlog. Some applicants have been told they'd have to wait ninety days or more!

And that's just about how long it took. Almost 3 months to the day. The results came simultaneously in the U.S. mail and electronically. Donny got his first. The 'Death Day' report predicted that he would meet his heavenly reward (never mind that he's an atheist, and who's to say he isn't going somewhere much warmer) on September 24th, 2091. His probable cause of death would be an aortic aneurysm. He quickly looked up what day that would be. Monday. Donny Vorhees was going to die on a Monday.

Great! He'd get to miss work! Then again, that's almost 52 years in the future. He might have a different job. Also included in the report was an offer from United Global for discounted life insurance. Anyway, as you might guess, the very next thing he did was call Ronny to see if he had gotten his report yet.

No luck. Ronny was still waiting. But, in a way, that was good. Apparently, their 'Death Day' information was being compiled by a different actuary. Not that they would violate work ethics, but now they could be sure there was no temptation on the part of the actuary to skip the hard work and just match them up because they were twins.

Minutes seemed like hours, hours like days, days like weeks and well, you get the idea. It felt to them like Ronny's prognosis was never going to show up. But, of course, it did.

At 6:27 P.M. Central time on November 27th, 2039, Ronny's report arrived. By coincidence, Donny happened to be at Ronny's house for dinner when the "you have mail" buzzer sounded on Donny's bionic arm. It read:

UNITED GLOBAL LIFE AND CASUALTY

11/27/2039

Dear Mr. Vorhees:

United Global Life and Casualty regret to inform you that, due to an unfortunate turn of events, a hermetically sealed package of blood, urine, and DNA samples sent to our laboratory in Great Falls, Montana, had been compromised and contaminated.

Your submissions were among those identified in this shipment. Therefore, we are unable to accurately ascertain the information you have requested regarding the date and probable cause of your demise.

In consideration of this ill-fated circumstance, United Global would like to respectfully submit propose that you re-submit your lab work to our medical staff. Or, if you choose, we will remit your monetary payment for services back into your account.

If you choose the former, please contact the Health Professional Technician in your area at the number listed below.

In the instance that you would like a refund, please contact us at the United Global service office at 1-800-727-9880 and cite case #162004. A refund will be credited to your account within 10 days.

We apologize for any inconvenience or stress this occurrence may have caused you and want to express our appreciation for your continued interest in the products and services of United Global Life and Casualty.

Yours Truly,

Madeline Swathmore

Madeline Swathmore
Vice President/Account Services.
P: 800-727-9800
E: M.Swathmore@UnitedGlobal.com

Well, that wasn't much fun! All that waiting, and now this! But, obviously, a refund was out of the question. Now, that Donny already received his 'Death Day' answers, they really wanted to know what Ronny's prognosis would be.

And so, for Ronny, it was back to being poked and swabbed and peeing in a cup, etc. etc. Given the situation, the lab promised that this time, they would expedite Ronny's physical panel work-up and his results would come back in record time.

So, true to the lab technician's word, Ronny waited just 10 days for United Globals' response. Before he opened the e-mail, he called his brother over to the house so they could open it together. Waiting for Donny to get over there, the suspense was nearly unbearable.

Alright! Now, the whole family gathered around while Ronny aimed the micro projector embedded in his arm up onto the wall. Mom, dad, wife, kids and brother Don. And so it began:

UNITED GLOBAL LIFE AND CASUALTY

12/14/2039

Dear Mr. Vorhees:

After a thorough review of your DNA, blood panel, urinalysis, ancestry, lifestyle questionnaire, and other relevant information, the underwriting department of United Global Life and Casualty has ascertained that barring an Act of God or perishing by your own hand, your last day of life will be September 24, 2091. The probable cause of your demise will be an aortic aneurysm.

We want to thank you for your patronage of United Global Life and Casualty and, as a gesture of our sincere appreciation, United Global Life and Casualty would like to offer you a discounted whole life insurance policy in any amount you choose.

With your permission, we will contact you in the near future to enquire about your interest in this life insurance proposal.

We at United Global Life and Casualty would like to congratulate you on the anticipated long duration of your future life.

Yours Truly,

Madeline Swathmore

Madeline Swathmore
Vice President/Account Services.
P: 800-727-9800
E: M.Swathmore@UnitedGlobal.com

Well damn! How about that! Born two minutes apart and leaving the 'above ground' portion of the planet on the same day 52 years in the future! Their 'Death Day' prognosis couldn't have been more similar. Could this be the promise for all identical twins? Will they die only two minutes apart? Well, we don't know that.

Anyway, with their prognosis reports now gone public, Donny and Ronny are famous celebrities. Public appearances, interview shows, a book deal, and more. And, they plan on having their 'Death Day' party every September 24th from now 'till....well, you know when.

See you in a bit.

"Confession"

WELL, DEAR FRIEND (we *are* friends by now, aren't we?) we all know that there is nothing that is a 'sure thing.' So, let us tell you the story of Mr. & Mrs. Jonathan Kier.

Charlene Kier lies in her hospital bed, miserable, and in all kinds of pain. She had applied for the United Global "Death Day" report and probable cause, some time ago, and true to their word, she was dying of end-stage kidney disease.

The prognosis report from United Global said her time on the top side of the grass would expire on May 25th, 2036. Today was May 14th. If they were right, and it sure looked like they were, she had just eleven more days to live.

Charlene's husband would come to visit by her side every day since she'd been hospitalized. He'd sit and hold her hand, professing undying (pun intended) love for her. Tears would sometimes well from his eyes knowing she would be gone from his life after 43 years of blissful wed. As they had no children, Jonathan would be looking at being alone for the rest of his 26 years. (He had purchased his own report)

Most of their almost four-and-a-half decades together were filled with love, affection, happiness, and good times. Charlene and Johnathan were a very religious couple. Still, like all relationships, and maybe especially a marriage, there were times of conflict. But here at the end of it all, it was simply a tragedy.

They were both somewhat comforted by their strong, Christian faith and belief that Charlene would soon be walking with Jesus.

But as her hour of death drew closer, Charlene became more unsettled. Not just about her terminal condition, there was something else.

When Jonathan arrived the next day, Charlene greeted him with her warmest smile and sat up in her hospital bed as well as she could muster.

As always, he pulled a chair next to her bed and grasped her hand lightly so as not to hurt her fragile bodily condition.

She began speaking almost immediately:

"Jonathan, my love, I need to speak with you!"

"Of course, sweetheart! Whatever you need! Talk to me!"

"Jonathan, I want to cleanse my soul before I meet Jesus!"

"Yes honey, I know."

"No Jonathan you don't know. This is about Bob."

"Bob? Who's Bob?"

"Our neighbor across the hall in the apartment building"

"Bob Santos?"

"Yes, my love, Bob Santos!"

"Well, what does he have to do with anything."

"Jonathan, please know that I love you and I have always loved you."

"I know that Char, but what's this about our neighbor Bob?"

"Sweetheart, before I go to meet Jesus, I need you to forgive me!"

"I do! I do forgive you! But what am I forgiving?"

"Jonathan, I'm so afraid. I'm afraid to tell you!"

"Tell me what?"

Taking a deep breath, tears welling in her eyes, Charlene let it out:

"Jonathan, I had an affair with Bob!"

"An affair? What do you mean by an affair?"

Charlene just stared at her husband. And that said it all.

Talk about a rock and a hard place. Here was his wife lying on her death bed, and this revelation is dropped on him like a bolt of sinister lightning from the sky. What should he do? How should he react? How could this be? An affair with their neighbor? When? How? How long?

"Please explain Char! Tell me what you mean!"

"Sweetheart, you were always gone off to golf with your buddies or on fishing trips or even church functions. I was so lonely. When I'd run into him in the hallway, he was always so nice to me. One morning while you were out golfing, he invited me in for coffee. It was all so innocent at first, and then...But it's over now Jonathan! It's been over for months! I realized it was so wrong! How could I betray you and our marriage? I love you so much. Please forgive me! Please! I need to cleanse my soul of this horrible thing I've done before I die and meet Jesus."

Jonathan unclasped his hand from Charlene's. Suddenly, Jesus and Heaven and all the rest of the religious crap weren't important anymore. How could this be? A double whammy! The love of his life is on her death bed telling him about an affair with the neighbor across the hall.

Tears began to roll down his cheeks. He was unable to speak. His tearing soon turned into painful sobs. His hands covered his face and fountains of tears soon crept through his closed fingers, streaming down over his hands onto his wrists.

Charlene watched this pitiful display of grief knowing it was her confession that brought it on her poor husband, and she, herself, began to cry uncontrollably.

Just then, a nurse walked into the room, making her rounds. Seeing this exhibition of mindless grief, she turned and walked right back out.

Finally, Jonathan was able to mouth three. simple, grief-stricken tear enveloped words:

"How could you?"

Charlene, let out a wail that brought the nurse back into the room. But one look at the scene and she ran right back out.

"How could you? Oh my God! How could you!"

(This is the part where Charlene realized she would have been better off taking her chances just talking to Jesus about it when she departed this Earth.)

Jonathan's knee-jerk reaction now was to just get up and leave the room. Spend some time with the revelation. But then things got worse. Or, better, depending on your point of view.

Before he could exit, the Nephrologist (that's a kidney doctor) came into the room flashing a smile big enough to light the moon.

"I have great news!" He declared.

Both Charlene and Jonathan just stared at him with their tear-soaked personas.

"What's wrong?" He asked.

Neither said anything.

"Well Charlene, you can both stop your crying. We found a matched donor kidney for you. We'll do surgery in the morning, and YOU are gonna live to be an old lady!"

The surgeon had never seen anyone look so sad with such good news. Both Charlene and Jonathan began crying with even more intensity. He considered they were tears of happiness and let it go at that.

"Alright! We'll get you prepped here tonight. No food until after the surgery tomorrow. You take care of yourself and congratulations."

And so, as it turned out, United Global was right and United Global was wrong. They had predicted Charlene's probable cause of death as kidney failure. But this time, the miracle of modern medicine got in the way. Well, as we pointed out: Nothing's perfect.

Now what?

The Surgeon left the room and Jonathan turned and stared at his previously dying wife. He paused for a moment, then turned again and headed for the door.

Charlene began the wailing again: *"Where is he going? Is he heading home to kill their neighbor Bob?"*

Jonathan didn't make it to the hospital for his wife's surgery the next morning. Instead, he flew down to the courthouse and filed divorce papers.

After the surgery. Charlene spent another week in the hospital recovering. She never heard a word from Jonathan, but a constable came to her room to serve her the divorce papers. Ironically, she was discharged on the very day United Global had predicted her passing.

Despite the divorce papers, she had hoped against hope that she would come home to find Jonathan there. Maybe not welcoming her with open arms, but maybe he would be there.

"Wouldn't he?"

The wheels keep turning at United Global Life and Casualty. Kerry Richmond was confounded and somewhat irritated that advances in medical technology kept interrupting and undoing his empirical personalized predictions. Meanwhile, the newly married Bob and Charlene Santos go to church together almost every Sunday.

"The Newly-Weds"

WELL, WE'VE ALL HEARD ABOUT 'love at first sight' haven't we? They say it's for real, but we've never known anyone who could verify that. However maybe it happened to you or someone you know. This next story is as close as we've come to witness the experience.

Rod Christiansen and Jeanette Swanson were teen-aged sweethearts. They met in the eighth grade and were an item all through high school and into college and beyond.

Supposedly they fell in love with each other from the very moment they swapped glances. There's good evidence of that, as they were inseparable. She was a classic beauty, and he was 'movie star' handsome. All the other guys knew she was 'off-limits' and their female counterparts didn't even try to come on to Rod. They knew he only had eyes for Jeanette. To him, she was a woman in a world full of girls.

After graduating college, Rod secured a job as an electrical engineer and Jeanette fulfilled her life-long dream of becoming an elementary school teacher.

As you might expect, it wasn't long before Rodney popped the question and Jeanette answered with the appropriately anticipated, *"Yes! Yes! Yes!"*

(Of course, it was *"Yes!"* what else could it be?)

Soon, they would be married and have the perfunctory little home in the country with a white picket fence and a little Rodney and a Jeanette and maybe even a Julianne (Her Grandmother's namesake).

They set the date for Saturday, May 23rd, 2037. It would be a gala affair and Jeanette's mom, (like all mothers of the bride) spent the entire year helping her only daughter prepare for the big day. The dress, the cake, the flowers the invitations, the whole shebang. Jeanette's father Randy wasn't as ebullient, as this wedding was hitting his checkbook pretty hard.

Rodney's parents were of very modest means, and they were quite satisfied with the tradition that the father of the bride picks up the tab for the glorious event. For his part, Randy figured that tradition expired decades ago, but the new in-laws weren't of a mind to contribute anything but their best wishes.

When the big day came, it went off without a hitch, just as mom had planned. It was a grand affair, with a hundred plus guests including friends, relatives, and business associates from both sides.

The music, dancing, and drunken happiness went on for hours until it was time for the new Mr. & Mrs. Christiansen to open their wedding gifts. Everyone cheered and applauded as each gift was unwrapped for the crowd to see.

As we might expect, there was Crystal, China, Flatware, Food processors, Big Screen TVs, dozens of cards with money, and one special gift from a rich uncle:

It came in a cream-colored, linen envelope secured with a red wax seal.

Inside, were two, embossed gift certificates; each, allocating the bearer to a United Global Life and Casualty actuarial report of their future 'Death Day.' Total value: $8,400.

When they opened the gift and announced the contents, the entire room fell silent.

Was this an appropriate wedding gift? Almost everyone attending the wedding knew what it was. The whole world had been talking about it for years!

But after the crowd digested the idea, with a few seconds' pause and some astonished looks exchanged among them, everyone started to applaud.

Viewed through the right window, this was an exceptional wedding present. For one thing, it was quite expensive and, both Rodney and Jeanette were only in their late twenties. Surely, they had another fifty-plus years of wedded bliss to look forward to.

Additionally, as the happy couple read the wording on the certificates out loud, it indicated that, if they chose not to exercise the option, the certificates were completely refundable. $8,400 was one hell of a generous gift.

"Thank you, Uncle Bob!"

The crowd applauded once more. This time with big enthusiasm.

And so, the evening ended, and Rod and Jeanette took off the next morning on their honeymoon to Jamaica; paid for by a group of Jeanettes' friends and work associates who all pitched in to make sure the newly-weds would have a magnificent beginning.

Between the embraces and kisses on the flight, Rod and Jeanette had a conversation about Uncle Bob's gift.

"What do you think babe? What should we do? Aren't you curious?"

"I don't know Rodney, I'm scared! And, $8400 is a lot of money. We could do a lot of things with that."

"I agree sweetheart, and maybe we should just 'take the money and run,' still, I'm curious as

thousands of people have paid for this. We can get it for free!

Rod and Jeanette pondered the idea all through their Jamaican honeymoon. Finally, they agreed they would do it. $8400 was a tidy sum of money, but certainly not a life changing fortune. When they arrived home, they set up an appointment with the United Global agent to go through the application process and see what was in store for their future.

They opted out of the online reports, choosing instead to receive their prognostications in the mail. Rod's arrived first. Just two weeks after they submitted their applications, his showed up, certified mail, in a big manila envelope.

Rod and Jeanette agreed that they would open their envelopes together in a ceremonial kind of thing. And so, with both Rod and Jeanette filled with anticipatory anxiety, his report remained unopened, sitting on top of the bedroom dresser while they waited for Jeanette's to arrive.

Can you imagine the apprehension they endured, with that envelope and all the information inside, just sitting there, gathering dust while they waited for Jeanette's to arrive?

In fact, Jeanette cheated a little. (Just a little) One day, while Rod was at work, and she was home alone. Jeanette couldn't stand it anymore. She 'steamed' open the envelope and peaked for just a moment at the contents inside. For her, it was a mystery no more. Rod was going to live a long and healthy life far into the future. She re-sealed the envelope and placed it right back in the exact place it sat before her clandestine chicanery.

It was almost three weeks of accumulated suspense before the second envelope arrived., addressed this time to Jeanette Christiansen.

They would open both envelopes together that night, with candles lit all around the great room in their new home. An unopened, chilled bottle of champagne sat on the coffee table awaiting a celebratory uncorking when the good news was revealed.

Rod went first. It was too late for second thoughts, but he almost wished they had never chosen this course of action.

But there it was. Rodney Christianson was destined to die on April 30th, 2105, of natural causes, 68 years from now, he would be 98 years old. They looked excitedly at each other, and Jeanette demonstrated her somewhat skilled acting abilities showing complete elated surprise. In his euphoria, Rod suspected nothing of his wife's previous deceit.

Now, it was her turn. Her hands shook violently as she opened the envelope. As she read the contents, tears began to escape themselves from the pools in her eyes.

This was no cause for celebration. Jeanette Christianson would be meeting her Maker on October 17th, 2044, just 6 short years from now, of a rare, esophageal disease, of which there is no known cure, called Achalasia.

Jeanette threw the papers down onto the floor and fell to her knees bawling, into the arms of her newly betrothed. There would be no celebratory champagne indulgence tonight.

They couldn't believe it! Now, both Rod and Jeanette cursed the day they decided to embark on this sinister informational journey. Six years! Not sixty, or even sixteen! She would be gone in just six years.

They quickly looked up the condition on the internet. Jeanette had already noticed that she had been experiencing some of the early symptoms. A sometimes inability to swallow her food. A nighttime cough. Dry eyes and a dry mouth.

She had been attributing these things to allergies when all along it was this Achalasia thing. Now, there would be no home in the country; no little Rodney or Jeanette, there would be nothing but 72 months of anxiety and pain and misery and then, death.

What would they do without each other?

Both Rod and Jeanette slept fitfully that night. In the morning, when cooler heads prevailed, they agreed that they would make the most of the time they had left together. They would travel and see the world. They would find ways to make every moment count; to love each other even more deeply.

By 2040, Jeanette's condition had become chronic. Though she had some good days, most were met with experiences of horrific pain and the accompanying misery.

But they kept their mutual promise to travel and make the most of their time together. Today, they found themselves beholding the magnificence of Grand Canyon National Park.

If you, yourself have ever visited this earthly wonder you will have noticed that Grand Canyon National Park is the perfect place to commit murder. Officials try to keep it quiet, but the simple fact is more than a few dozen individuals die from falls into the Canyon every year.

There are no guard railings protecting tourists from the Canyon's edge, and there are no video cameras surveying the area. If someone were standing close enough, a little 'nudge' in the wrong direction would send them down hundreds of feet to the rocky bottom.

As the months after the revelation went on, Jeanette Christiansen learned to love her husband more than she thought possible. Rod too was enveloped with loving emotions for his dying wife.

But love sometimes comes in varying flavors, and jealousy is often a sinister companion. What consumed Jeanette these days was the thought of her demise and Rod moving on with another lover, replacing her in his life. After all, he had many long decades ahead. What were the chances he wouldn't find her replacement?

And so, in a delirious fit of emotional desperation and jealousy, Standing directly behind him as he stood on the precipice of the Canyon, gazing down at the chasm, Jeanette, looking around and seeing no other soul in the vicinity, closed her eyes and gave a gentle push, propelling her husband down into the deep crevice of Grand Canyon National Park.

Immediately as it happened, intense remorse came over her, she fell to her knees and screamed and wailed and cried as a crowd gathered to see what had happened.

Such an accident! Her husband tripped and fell down the Canyon to his death. Yet another, Grand Canyon National Park yearly statistic.

"Oops!" Jeanette was inconsolable! Her love for him would never die. But he would. (Her too)

"Until death do us part."

"You first Rodney!"

15

"This'll Kill Ya!"

THIS TIME, I NEED TO TELL YOU about a fellow I never knew but read about. His name was Charles Johnson.

Charles was your stereotypical, middle-class family man who, like thousands of others these days, decided to pay the money to see how long it would be before he was counted among the 'dearly- departed.'

Just two weeks later, the documents came back from United Global happily informing Mr. Johnson that he could look forward to another sixty-four years of continuous bliss. He would die on September 29th, 2101, at the ripe old age of 104!

This made Charles (and his family and friends) exuberant! Sixty-four years seemed like forever. But the 'bliss' part wasn't going to be included in the forever package.

One late evening, there were loud knocks on the door, accompanied by shouts yelling *"Police! Open up!"* This, of course, woke Charles' entire family. What could this be about?

Half asleep, with his wife trailing close behind, Charles stumbled to the front door and opened it wide to see three policemen, in Kevlar vests, guns drawn, and several police cruisers parked right up on his driveway and lawn. White, red, and blue lights flashed back and forth everywhere.

Taking it all in through the sleep still in his eyes, Charles couldn't help but notice, all the houses on the block, with porch lights on and neighbors peering out their windows at the commotion up the street.

Before Mr. Johnson could speak, the sergeant at the front of the law enforcement trio spoke loudly into his face:

"Mr. Charles Maurice Johnson?"

"Uh, yes! What's this about?"

"You are hereby under arrest for the murder of Carolyn M. Carson!"

The cop then proceeded to read him his Miranda rights.

"You have the right to remain silent....."

With that, Charlie Johnson was handcuffed and taken away to one of the cruisers, presumably to jail, while his wife and young children all stood at the door in silent astonishment!

There'd be no sleep for Mrs. Johnson tonight. The children slept fitfully.

"Who the hell is Carolyn Carson?"

Early the next morning, Nancy Johnson immediately called the police.

"Hello! My name is Nancy Johnson. Last night my husband Mr. Charles Johnson was arrested and taken away. Can you please tell me where he's incarcerated?"

"Yes Ma'am! Mr. Johnson is in custody in the 12th precinct. Would you like me to transfer you to their information officer?"

"Yes! Yes! Please!"

"One moment!"

Once transferred to the correct precinct HQ, Nancy Johnson learned that her husband was indeed in custody and, that she could come and visit him. But considering the seriousness of the alleged offense, Mr. Johnson was considered a flight risk, and his bond was set at one million dollars.

Now, whether or not you, yourself have ever been incarcerated, you probably know that whatever the bail bond is set, you only have to put up 10% of the money in order to be released. That's the good news. The bad news is that in the case of Mr. Johnson, that was $100,000! The Johnson family didn't have that kind of money, except in Mr. Johnson's IRA.

That was troubling in itself, but before anything, Nancy had to get down to the police station to speak with her betrothed. She called her mother to come and watch the little ones while she drove to the destination.

The officer who escorted her to the visitor's room was very nice and mannerly, but the environment itself was very intimidating for someone who had never been in trouble of any kind with law enforcement. The visitor's 'room' was more like an 8x10 cubicle with a metal table and two chairs on either side. There was a big, mirror-like, window on the left wall and Nancy considered that it was probably one of those two-way contraptions like she saw on TV crime dramas.

After a short while, Charles was led into the room by a burly, gruff-looking guard. Charles' eyes were withdrawn with deep, dark bags, and he was shackled on both his wrists and ankles.

Nancy let out a gasp. She was taken aback by his disheveled appearance, and especially by the shackles. She didn't know what to expect, but it wasn't this.

They were given fifteen minutes. Obviously, he needed a bail bondsman and an attorney. Not necessarily in that order. Nancy asked him: *"Where will we get the bond money?"*

Charles asked her if her parents could find the money and lend it to them until this thing was over. She replied that she wasn't sure. Her parents were of very modest means.

Barring that, he would pull the money out of his IRA and worry about the penalties later. With the bond and attorney discussion out of the way, it was time to ask:

"Charles! Who is this, Carolyn Carson?"

Uh Oh! With all the sincerity he could muster Charles said:

"Nancy! She was just a work associate. A friend. I don't know what this is all about."

(It was a little white lie, but this was no time to go into detail)

"Well, my God Charles! Why would they think you had anything to do with her death?"

"I have no idea. I'm as confused as you are honey."

Fifteen minutes went by in a whisper. The guard came in and broke up the conversation. As her husband hobbled out of the room in his chains, Mrs. Johnson resolved to find a way to get the bond money and a good criminal attorney.

Meanwhile, Charles languished in jail while she went to work on it.

As they say: *"When it rains it pours!"* Nancy's parents were living on Social Security but had $19,000 in savings they would be happy to provide. Nancy refused the offer. She found a criminal attorney with five-star reviews and made an appointment to meet with him. He'd be happy to represent her husband but needed a $25,000 retainer. Now Charles would have to tap $125k from his IRA. Nancy visited Charles almost every day. Every time she came to visit, she'd bring more documents to be signed to extract the IRA money. Sadly, this would take his retirement savings down to just $5,634.00.

Finally, after- two-and-a-half long weeks, she secured the funds, paid the attorney the retainer, and got Charles released on bail.

There was a dark, emotional cloud hanging over them. On the way home in the car, Nancy began grilling Charles about things.

Apparently, Carolyn Carson had been strangled to death in her apartment more than a month ago. It was on the news, but it didn't make the headlines. Pittsburgh was a big city, and these things happen all too regularly. It was nothing special. After an internet search, Charles found the story but tried to ignore it.

"But why do they suspect you, Chuck?" (He hated that she always called him Chuck.)

"Chuck" didn't answer. He just stared straight ahead with a non-descript look on his face."

Then, abruptly he blurted out: *"They found my DNA at the murder scene!"*

Nancy was awe struck. She momentarily turned toward him and asked:

'Your DNA! How could that be? Where did they get your DNA? And why would it be at her apartment anyway?"

He answered with a feeble grimace:

"Apparently, my DNA was in the national database. Remember, I submitted a DNA swab when I applied for the United Global Life and Casualty actuarial program! These days, any DNA submitted to any organization or government body is logged on the national database. I hadn't thought of that when I made my application and lab work."

"Well, ok! But how did your DNA get in her apartment?"

"Uh, well, it seems I visited her apartment a time or two."

Now, obviously confused, Nancy asked:

"A time or two? What does that mean? A time or two?"

And, in a very monotone, matter of fact, almost whisper, 'Chuck' uttered:

"Honey, it means we were having an affair!"

With those words, Mrs. Nancy Johnson slammed on the brakes in such a violent way it pushed them both forward into their respective seat belts; and in a chilling screech that would almost wake the dead, screamed in his face: Whaat? What did you say? You were having an affair?"

Charles knew this would come to light at some point anyway. "Might as well get it all out now."

Cars behind them were honking their horns incessantly, but Nancy Johnson ignored everything around her and just laid her head on the steering wheel bawling intensely with the pain of her husband's newly disclosed betrayal.

Charles continued:

"It wasn't exactly an affair Babe! And I'm not the one who killed her! I have no idea what happened to her. Who she was with, what she was doing. I swear I have no idea!"

Those words were of little comfort to Nancy Johnson. Forget the murder, and everything connected. Chuck's revelation of the affair was all consuming. This whole nightmare was more than she could bear, and now he gives her this reality sandwich.

She lifted her head from the steering wheel, pushed the vehicle's button to "autonomous driving" and let it drive them home.

The children were beyond excited to see their Daddy, but no words were exchanged for hours between Nancy and Charles Johnson.

Finally, it was bedtime. She would have preferred he sleep downstairs on the couch but didn't push it. He crawled into bed and attempted to put his arm around her. She didn't try to remove it but laid on her side away from him sobbing herself to sleep.

Charles thought to himself: *"Damn! Why did I ever apply for that Goddamned United Global thing? Nobody else ever got my DNA!"*

In the morning, he would meet with his attorney, Andrew Brodkey. They would begin the discussion of his defense. The court date was set for June 24th. 36 days away.

After the niceties were exchanged. Andrew Brodkey got down to the uncomfortable conversation.

"Charles! I'm your attorney. I'm the one person you don't want to lie to. If I don't know the whole truth about what happened, it will be impossible for me to successfully defend you. First question: Were you having an affair with Ms. Carson?"

Nancy Johnson sat right next to Charles, and even though it *'kind of'* came out yesterday in the car, it was still very awkward making the admission to his attorney.

Sensing the delicate moment, the attorney suggested that Mrs. Johnson leave the room, just for a minute or two. She too, thought it was a good idea.

Once the two were alone, Charles spilled it all out. He had been seeing Carolyn Carson for a couple of years. Though they tried to keep it a secret, just about everyone at work was wise to their shenanigans, and that's probably how the authorities found out about it. Combine their love affair with his prolific DNA all over the crime scene, and Mr. Charles Johnson was in deep doo-doo.

"Next question! Did you do it?"

For a moment, the silence was, as they say, *deafening.* There was a virtual stare-down between Mr. Johnson and Andrew Brodkey, Esq. Attorney at law.

After what seemed like an eternity. Charles, shaking his head back and forth and flailing his arms up over his head, took a deep breath, and half mumbled:

"It was an accident!"

His attorney's face, now completely devoid of emotion asked:

"So! You accidentally strangled her?"

"Well not exactly. Carolyn loved rough sex. She liked being choked until she'd almost pass out. She would eg., me on. She would say "Harder! Harder! But this time it went too far. I thought she had just passed out, but I wasn't able to revive her. After almost half an hour of trying CPR and anything else I could think of, I panicked and left the apartment with her lying there in bed naked. I went home and kept telling myself that it didn't really happen and that she'd wake up sometime in the night and I'd see her at work the next day. But that didn't happen. I went back the next morning, hoping against hope that I'd find

her sitting up or making breakfast, but when I got there, she was still lying in the same place on the bed, staring up at the ceiling." Two days later it was on the news wire and on TV. They had found her nude body and suspected foul play.I thought I had removed any traces of my being there, but I forgot a month earlier I had given a sample of my DNA to United Global Life and Casualty for one of those 'Death Day' things.

"Don't beat yourself up too badly for that one Mr. Johnson, the authorities would have found you anyway. When something like this happens, the first place they look is the person or persons closest to the victim. Then, they work their way outward from there. With or without the DNA, they would have discovered you were in an intimate relationship with Ms. Carson, and you'd have been a prime suspect. So! Do we plead guilty or not guilty? We can strategize either way, but I need you to decide. If you plead guilty, we can cop a reduced sentence, perhaps Manslaughter, which, after we're finished, you're incarcerated for ten to fifteen years, out in seven with good behavior. Or we can go the other way and see if we can get a sympathetic judge and jury. Maybe you want to think it over?"

"Well, if I plead "not guilty" do you think you can get me out of this mess?"

"Maybe! There's a lot of evidence against you, but I enjoy challenges."

"Ok then. It's not guilty. What do we do next?"

"Next, we find out who did the crime."

"Who did it? What do you mean?"

"Well, it wasn't you!"

That statement took Charles aback. He wasn't sure he heard it right. He shook his head In total confusion and blurted out:

"It wasn't?"

"Nope. I'll start the investigation tomorrow. We'll find out who did this. For right now, please just go home and relax. I'll be in touch."

Charles' wife hadn't come back into the room yet, but now, she opened the door and asked if they were finished.

Weeks passed. At the pre-trial hearing, Charles pleaded *"Not Guilty."* Finally, the jury selection was completed, and the trial would begin as scheduled.

Attorney Andrew Brodkey put on a masterful defense. He demonstrated to the jury that their investigation found that Ms. Carson enjoyed 'rough sex' And (much to the surprise of Mr. Johnson and the prosecution.) that while, Carolyn Carson was, indeed, having an affair with Mr. Johnson, further investigation showed that she was also seeing various other men, any one of whom could have been the killer. Their DNA was also found all over Ms. Carson's apartment. . Simply put, Carolyn

Carson was a sex addict who enjoyed the idea of choking during intercourse. So, why did the police hone in on Mr. Johnson? The others had alibis, but Mr. Johnson had one of his own. Under testimony, Mrs. Johnson had confirmed that Charles was home that evening by 9:30 p.m. The coroner had ascertained that death occurred to Ms. Carson sometime between 9 and 10 p.m.

Could he possibly have strangled the woman, got dressed, and arrived home all in the course of just 30 minutes? Not impossible but, improbable.

In fact, that's exactly what happened. When he couldn't revive his lover, Charles was frozen with fear. If there were Olympic medals given out for the fastest time putting clothes back on, running away, and speeding toward home, Charles would have won the gold!

However, Andrew Brodkey reminded the jury that the 'Burden of proof' was on the State, not the defendant and if any 'reasonable doubt' entered their perception of his guilt, they would have to find him 'Not Guilty.'

He only needed one juror of the twelve to see things his way and Mr. Johnson would have at least a mis-trail or be acquitted.

The jury deliberated only 4 hours until they delivered the verdict to the judge.

Charles stood nervous and silent next to his attorney as they read the verdict:

"On the count of second-degree murder, we the jury, find the defendant, Charles Maurice Johnson, Not Guilty!"

Charles' knees buckled and he collapsed into the arms of his most competent attorney.

Mrs. Johnson sitting directly behind them put her hands to her face and cried into her handkerchief.

Now, all was right with the world. Just as the United Global actuary report stated: Mr. Charles M. Johnson could now look forward to another sixty-four years of a quiet, sedate, satisfying domestic life. He would no longer have to worry about spending the bulk of those years in prison with his new boyfriend 'Bubba.'

Except:

- Mrs. Johnson would now be filing for divorce. She had lost her sense of humor concerning the affair.

- He could pay child support and see the kids on weekends.

- With all the commotion and high-profile press coverage around the case, Pittsburgh State Bank was forced to terminate Charles' Vice Presidency.

- Andrew Brodkey's well-earned attorneys' fees amounted to a total of $276,000 not, including $27.84 for document copies, $38.97 for postage, and $345 in court fees,

- This would force his bankruptcy. He would now be making $17.50 an hour stocking shelves at Walmart with a chance for advancement to the assistant manager if he worked hard and was a team player.

- 64 years, 768 months, 3,328 weeks, 23,360 days, 560,640 hours and 33,638,400 minutes of miserable, United Global Life and Casualty actuarial life left to live. All this and with a claimed 98.6% United Global Life and Casualty accuracy.

The judge exclaimed: *"Congratulations Mr. Johnson, you are free to go!"*

Charles Maurice Johnson thought to himself: *"Go where?"*

16

"All Mixed Up"

As we explained when we first got together, United Global Life didn't' have the 'Death Day Prognosis Project actuarial program until Kerry Richmond developed it in 2035.

Upon hearing about it, a person we once knew named Richard Blanchett, was immediately intrigued, but he didn't have the funds on hand to pursue his interest.

Finally, in 2038, saving every nickel and dime towards his goal, he had enough cash to purchase the base program (though, not the extra $750 for probable cause. He went online and scheduled an appointment for the required lab and application documents.

His wife was against the idea from the beginning and told him so, but Richard was consumed with the idea of knowing the day of his demise. For her part, she could have cared less. In fact, she didn't want to know hers *or* his! Better to keep it a mystery as nature intended.

The customary two weeks went by and then, there it was. It first came electronically and was followed quickly by the hard copy in the mail slot. Anxiously, Richard opened the electronic report and quickly scanned down to the important parts. With that, he was immediately struck with remorse that he had ever embarked on this curious journey.

Mr. Richard Blanchett was going to pass from this world on December 12th, 2038, just four short months from then, for cause unknown.

Panic ensued. Richard's hands started shake uncontrollably. This wasn't at all what he expected. The whole idea of this thing was just a lark. "Be careful what you wish for."

Find out what's wrong with me. Maybe we can fix it.

"Oh my God! What do I do? How do I tell Barbara? This can't be true! Maybe they're wrong! It's not 100%! What could possibly be wrong with me? I'm healthy! Well, I thought I was healthy! Christ! What will my family do? We have no savings! No life insurance! Ok! Ok! Calm down! I'll call Doctor Quinlan right now! Make an appointment."

When he called, he informed the receptionist that he needed to see the doctor right away. It was an emergency. She told him to call 911 or go to the Emergency Room.

That wouldn't do. He needed to see the doctor ASAP!

The receptionist was taken aback by his intensity and decided not to fight his demands.

"I have a cancellation this afternoon at 3 p.m. Can you make it then Mr. Blanchett?"

"Yes! Yes! That's perfect. I'll be there at three. Thank you very much!"

Richard drove like thunder to the doctor's office, running stop signs, red lights, intersections, and everything in between.

He arrived at 2:30 p.m. A little early, he knew, but maybe the doctor could get him in ahead of schedule. He was right.

Once in Doctor Quinlan's office, he explained everything to him about the 'Death Day' actuarial report. If they were right, and it was almost 100% guaranteed they were, he would be dead in four short months.

Like Ronald Osborne's cardiologist back in chapter 10, Richard's doctor was incredulous.

Like almost everyone on the planet, he was well aware of the United Global actuarial program, but most health care professionals, including himself, were extremely skeptical and even irate that this purported 'scam' was proliferating in society. These days, he was booked solid with patients who had signed up for the same thing and wanted assurances they were "ok"! They were keeping the radiology departments very busy.

Doctor Quinlan assured Richard he was just fine, still, the doctor had an extremely nervous patient sitting in front of him. Just to cover himself, he would have to run a battery of tests, beginning with a blood panel. He'd also order up an MRI, CAT SCAN and whatever else in the event something terminal truly *had* invaded his patient. Richard Blanchett did not look like he was going to terminate anytime soon.

His doctor's assurance was some comfort to Richard, but still, he was spooked. He hadn't expected this! Didn't even share the report with his wife yet, but she'd be asking about it soon. Worry, worry, worry:

"What if this is real? I'll leave my wife and two kids behind with no income. How are they gonna survive?"

Days went by. The doctor called with the blood panel and urinalysis. Both were perfect.

He looked to be a healthy specimen of a forty-two-year-old male. Also, the CAT Scan was clean. Nothing there. Perhaps the MRI would turn something up. But the report hadn't come back yet.

As I mentioned a few paragraphs earlier, those radiology guys were very busy.

Richard was in a quandary. There was no way his family could survive financially if he was gone. He wasn't proud of the fact that he hadn't saved anything in the event of a catastrophe, but it was what it was.

For himself, he just had to find a way to make sure they'd be "ok" in the event of his demise. But how?

This was a man who had never even had a traffic ticket. Law-abiding, home, work, and church. But now, he found himself planning a sinister plot to execute a robbery. If he secured enough money from the job, maybe his family would be ok when he died. It wouldn't be easy. In the old days, you could walk into a bank or even a Walmart and pull a *"Stick 'em up!"* but nowadays, everything is digital. How do you rob digital? It could be done if you were adept at hacking digital wallets, but that wasn't one of Richard's skills.

Still, he had a gun, and just a few miles away, there was a gold and silver dealer in a strip mall. That was the ticket! He would survey the area for days and make note of the slowest period when others weren't around. He'd also make note of the closing time. Just before they closed shop for the day, he would walk up to the store and clandestinely spray the video camera outside with black paint. Then, he would push the security buzzer, quickly pull on a ski mask, point the gun at the clerk inside and begin to alleviate the store of its contents. There would be hundreds of thousands if not a million dollars in gold, silver, and collectibles in every corner of that shop.

That's what he would do. And when the day came, It was just as he had planned. When he pulled up to the shop, Richard was nervous as hell, but still determined to execute things. The ski mask was tucked into his back pocket. His handgun was concealed in his front right pocket. The spray can of black paint sat beside him waiting to perform its part of the operation. Store closing was 5 p.m. Almost twilight this time of year. In just 3 minutes, we'll let the games begin.

He had parked his vehicle a couple of doors down from the shop so as not to be obvious or have it videoed before he got the chance to block out the camera. One more look around outside. Nobody in sight in either direction. He emerged from the car as stealthily as he knew how, casually walked up to the front door, and sprayed the camera hanging out front. No backing out now. The criminality had begun. He then pushed the access button.

Inside, the clerk's job was to assess if the person buzzing the door was a threat before pressing the entry release. But looking at the man standing twenty feet away from his position behind the sales counter, Richard looked credible enough. He had not yet donned the ski mask.

A last-minute customer would be welcome. Business had been slow as of late.

As he swung the door open, Richard simultaneously pulled the ski mask over his head and brandished his firearm. In the most aggressive and vicious voice, he could muster Richard gave the clerk a command:

"Don't you even THINK about pushing an alarm button! Come out from around the counter!"

Looking at the 9mm Glock pistol staring him in the face, the clerk had no intention of being a hero. Yyyessir! His arms went straight up in surrender as he nervously shuffled over and around the sales case.

Richard gruffly bellowed: *"Ok now! Where do you keep the gold?"*

"The Gold?"

"Yes, the gold! Where do you keep the gold?"

"Well, there's some right here in the case sir!
Terrified, the young man nervously uttered:

"Ppplease don't shoot me!"

The gun was starting to shake convulsively in Richard's hand, scaring Hell out of the clerk. To his own surprise, Richard's voice was now permeated with nervousness, frustration, and anger: *"That's not enough! Where's the big stuff?"*

In a petrified screech that approached falsetto, the frightened clerk responded:

"It's in the back sir. In the safe."

"Let's get it!"

The clerk just stood there, hands in the air, frozen in place.

With everything going his way so far, Richard was starting to get a hang for this robbery business. He would take strong command of the situation.

"NOW!"

That did the trick. Timidly, the young man turned and walked towards the back of the shop

Richard followed closely pushing his weapon into the soft folds of the young man's back.

Richard's body was jam-packed with flowing adrenaline. The whole experience felt surreal and dream-like. Still, the die had been cast and at this point, there was no turning back.

"Open it!"

Richard knew the clerk would claim he didn't have the combination. He was also sure he did. As the young man attempted to spit out those very words, Richard simply interrupted:

"Don't give me some song and dance about not knowing the combination. If you don't open it right now, I swear I'll shoot you dead right here."

Of course, Richard had never hurt anyone in his entire life and surely wouldn't really shoot the kid, would he? Still, you never know. Richard was really getting into character taking on the persona of a hardened criminal. Almost enjoying the bullying, he was exacting on his detainee.

As we said earlier, the clerk had no intention of being a hero. Hands trembling, he worked the combination and the door to the safe swung open to reveal at least 20 or 30 gleaming gold bars stacked one on top of the other. Below the bars were shelves of rare gold and silver coins. This was the mother lode.

Two large black briefcases sat inconspicuously to the side. Apparently, they'd be used in the event of transporting the bullion to other locations. Richard instructed his captive to fill both cases with the entire contents of the safe.

The young man did as he was told but both cases were filled to the brim and still, more treasure remained inside the safe. Richard quickly judged a half-million or more was piled into the cases. That would have to do. He still had to carry the booty to his vehicle. It would be heavy.

With his pistol, Richard motioned for his hostage to carry the two containers to the front of the store. Grappling with the handles, he picked up the heavy plunder and wobbled back and forth until he breathlessly reached the front of the store and set them down.

From there, Richard would carry them to his vehicle parked a few doors down.

He was relieved to see that darkness had fallen. It would make his escape that much easier.

"Ok now! Push the button and open the door and set the briefs on the doorstep."

It was almost over. Calmer now, Richard's hands that held his weapon were no longer quivering. Still, he held the gun on the shop clerk, ensuring he would not try to escape as he picked up the heavy cases once more and slid them out the door.

"Now! Lie face down on the floor and count to one hundred! Don't even think about getting up until you've finished counting."

Now, with immense effort, Richard picked up the overloaded containers and lugged them to his escape vehicle, struggling mightily, he heaved them separately into the trunk.

Meanwhile, the terrorized shop clerk knew full well his captor could not get back into the store. He immediately rose up from the floor and observing the perpetrator's car and license plate as it left the scene. He called the police.

For his part, Mr. Richard Blanchett drove away with a trunk loaded down with a treasure trove of gold and silver bullion. Surely enough to support his wife and kids for a very long time after he was gone. And no one got hurt! He never even needed to fire his pistol. He was feeling the succinct pleasure of the effects of endorphins flowing through his extremities.

When he arrived at his house, his vehicle was lopsided with the backside almost scraping on the ground from the weight of the treasure he'd just absconded.

The gun and ski mask were on the passenger seat right next to him.

As he walked into the kitchen from the garage door he happily exclaimed:

"Honey, I'm home!"

Hearing his voice, Julie, filled with emotion about all his recent medical chaos, ran to him throwing her arms around him with a hug that practically knocked him over!

"Babe! Where have you been? You're never late coming home from work! Why didn't you call? A certified letter came in the mail for you today. I signed for it. I didn't open it, but. It looks important."

Richard looked around the area to make sure the kids weren't nearby.

"Ok, I'll read it in a moment. But first, we need to talk about something!"

"Uh.ok! What is it honey?"

"Sweetie, you know that United Global thing I signed up for a while ago?"

"Yes, did you get the report back? Are you going to live forever?"

"Well, that's the problem, it appears I'm not going to live much longer. In fact,

If they're correct, I have only a few more weeks left on this planet!"

"What? That can't be! I also forgot to tell you; Doctor Quinlan called earlier. Your MRI came back negative! There's nothing wrong with you Richard!"

"Seriously? I don't know how that can be!"

"It's what he said, Richard. You're in perfect health."

"Let me see that letter, Julie."

His wife got up off the sofa and retrieved the certified letter.

"Here you are sweetheart."

Richard gingerly opened the letter and began to read.

UNITED GLOBAL LIFE AND CASUALTY

November 19, 2038

Mr. Richard Blanchette
1919 Sycamore Lane, Cleveland, Ohio.

Dear Mr. Blanchette:

As you are most likely aware, we at United Global had received an application for an actuarial report on your proposed "Death Day" application.

Regrettably, an egregious error has occurred as there were two distinctly separate Richard Blanchette's who had filed a Prognosis Project tuarial application on the same day and were processed at the same time in our laboratories.

In essence, your reports were somehow interchanged at the fulfillment department, and you received the report for Mr. Richard Blanchette of St. Charles, Missouri and he, in turn. received yours.

Subsequently, your correct actuarial report is attached. We apologize for any inconvenience or anxiety this may have caused you.

As a gesture of compensation for this complication, we at United Global would like to extend an offer of 20-year term life at a deeply discounted rate.

Please let us know if you have an interest in this compensatory proposal.

Sincerely,

Madeline Swathmore

Madeline Swathmore
Vice President/Account Services.
P: 800-727-9800
E: M.Swathmore@UnitedGlobal.com

After reading the letter, Richard Blanchette looked up at his wife with deep sadness on his face. How could he tell her he had just pulled off an armed robbery?

In the next minutes, two police cruisers arrived in the drive-way. They were looking for a dark blue, 2035 Chevrolet EV. with a license plate registered to a Mr. Richard Blanchette, 1919 Sycamore Lane, Clevland, Ohio.

The actuarial report stated that Richard Blanchette of Cleveland, Ohio would live to be a ripe old age.

It didn't say what kind of life it would be.

His family visits him almost every Sunday and on holidays.

17

"Those Golden Years!"

YOU KNOW, AFTER ALL THESE STORIES, we think the boys and girls over at United Global need to get more organized. For sure, they're tripping over their wallets with this 'Prognosis Project' thing, Kudos to Kerry Richmond, but mistakes like that Blanchette fiasco is wreaking havoc on some nice (and some not-so-nice) people. Don't you think? Here's another one:

John and Jody Ragsdale were a docile, elderly couple living in South-West Iowa. They'd been married for 45 years, never had any kids, and, neither John nor Jody were very sophisticated financially. Jody was a high school graduate and John had quit school in the tenth grade.

Now, in their supposed "Golden Years" they had no IRA or savings except their monthly Social Security payments. And so, to supplement their income, at the age of seventy-two John worked at a local convenience store, and Jody, just a shade younger, worked behind the counter putting together orders at the Soup-or-Sub sandwich shop. Workdays weren't so bad for Jody at the Soup-or-Sub, but the newly promoted manager at John's convenience store was on an 'Adolph Hitler School of Etiquette' power trip, ordering his subordinates to perform menial tasks like cleaning restrooms with barked-out, demeaning shouts in front of customers. John would come home almost every night physically exhausted and emotionally beaten up. All this for $22 digital dollars an hour.

Still, John and Jody knew how to have fun. Once a month, when the social security checks came in, they found themselves at the casino, pushing the buttons on the penny slot machines. They almost never won. Then one night, Jody lifted her now-cramped index finger for the 837th time and pressed down hard.

Suddenly, all the stars in the sky became perfectly aligned; the moon went blue, and its beams flew in all directions, abandoning their usual orderly sequence.

John and Jody Ragsdale had just hit, what was affectionately called "The Progressive Penny Jackpot!" Nineteen million, two hundred twenty-four thousand, six hundred eighteen dollars and twenty-seven cents! ($19,224,618.27)

At first, they didn't see it! But the machine made so much noise, they knew *something* was going on. Soon, a crowd gathered, and casino management and security hurried to their slot location. It was breathtaking! Casino management soon verified that they, indeed, had won the 'Progressive.' But of course, that kind of money would have to be extracted from the Casino hold.

"Could they please come back tomorrow to retrieve their digital winnings and pose for pictures with casino executives?"

That was not a problem.

John asked: "Absolutely! What time works best?"

Naturally, sleep eluded them both that night. Every gambler's dream is to hit the big one, and tonight, John and Jody Ragsdale literally beat the odds.

When they arrived at the casino the next day, a host met them at the entrance and ushered them down to the entertainment stage. There were balloons and crepe paper and party hats and more. In addition, there were TV cameras, news crews, and of course, the photographer.

As expected, the casino had already constructed a five-foot-long, three-foot-high facsimile of a digital checking account with their names emblazoned on the front.

By noon today, they would be famous. And that, dear reader friend, was the problem.

As we explained at the beginning of this chapter, John and Jody were not financially sophisticated. They didn't know to seek out a financial advisor or tax attorney. All they knew was, that they were almost $20 million dollars richer. The casino immediately took the State tax out of the winnings but left it up to John and Jody and the IRS to work out the rest.

They did know enough to deposit the multi-million-dollar digital token in their bank. And, to their separate amazement, the personal banker treated them entirely differently than she had ever done before.

Jody thought: *"Could it be because of the money?"* (Duh!)

As we might expect, both John and Jody bid farewell to their jobs. John's conversational departure with the new convenience store manager didn't really follow the polite protocol; I'll spare you the details and leave the back-and-forth dialogue to your imagination.

So now that all the dust had settled, John proposed an idea to Jody: They had both heard about that United Global Life and Casualty thing. (Who didn't?) John suggested they purchase a report for each of them individually. Since John was going on 73 years and Jody was not far behind, he wanted to see how much time they had left. In 2036, an adult male could expect to live 88.4 years. A female even longer.

In any event, they visited the global insurance agent, submitted their lab work and questionnaires, and sat and waited for the results. Voila! Three anxiety-filled weeks later they arrived. John would live to be 91 and Jody 96. Perfect! Death Day, John Ragsdale, September 29th, 2053. Jody, September 30th, 6 years later.

Thank you to Kerry Richmond and those nice people at Untied Global Life and Casualty.

They knew exactly what they would do. Apparently dreams come true.

John would now draw out a million in digital cash and purchase the 'Top-of-the-line' autonomous EV motorhome with all the bells and whistles.

They would spend the next 20 years just traveling everywhere in their 'state of the art' motorhome. With all the money they would ever need or want, and plenty of years left to spend it, those golden years had finally arrived. For the next 18 months, life on the road for John and Jody Ragsdale was gloriously wonderful. Until one day in early 2038.

An e-mail came across the motor home computer. It was a greeting from the IRS. Apparently, with all the excitement when they won the jackpot, they had neglected to pay their Federal Taxes on the winnings. Of course, the casino reported the winnings, and the Feds wanted their share. This was disconcerting, but even now, the Ragsdale's were not big spenders. There would still be millions left after they gave the Gov. its share. But then things went from bad to worse.

Remember earlier when we told you about the pictures they took at the casino? Well, that big, fat, five-foot-long check with their names written all over it didn't go unnoticed by the criminal element. It took a little while, but, once the thieves captured their names eventually the hackers were able to acquire enough personal information, to access the Ragsdale's bank account. Social Security numbers, passwords, codes, and facial recognition from the casino pictures, allowed entry to the Ragsdale's bank account and the millions stored within. $13,664,000 was now in the hands of Russian Cyber Criminals. They were nice enough to leave $312.12.

The Ragsdale's' were traveling through Tennessee and pulled up to a charging station in a campground, motor home lodge near Nashville. Tomorrow, they would visit the Grand Old Opry!

Jody got out her I-phone 23 'Lightning' and flipped to the bank account "Q Code" to pay for the motorhome EV charge. $289.50 went through. Thank You!

Then she went inside the campground office to pay for two-nights lodging. And that's when the nightmare began. This time, her "Q Code" was declined. If you've ever been in earshot when someone had their credit card declined, you already know that Jody Ragsdale said what everyone says: *"There must be some mistake!"*

But there wasn't.

Frantic calls, e-mails, and texts to the Menlo, Iowa State Bank went unheeded. They had no choice but to head back home to straighten this mess out.

You may wonder: *"Isn't the bank liable for the attack on the Ragsdale's account?"*

The short answer is: *"Nope."*

For one thing, a 'State Bank' losing millions in assets would easily bankrupt them. But, more importantly, these hackers did it all by the book, even down to facial recognition to verify the account. For sure, the FBI would follow up, but to make matters worse, this was a foreign entity who cleaned out the account. Most likely Russians. How are they gonna get to Russians? Those millions were gone, and John and Jody no longer have the resources, sophistication, or where- with- all to get them back.

They did manage to sell their 'used' motor home for $225k digital.   But the IRS soon absconded with those funds. So, for Progressive Penny Jackpot winners John and Jody Ragsdale, it was a nice ride (no pun intended) but they're spending those golden years that United Global Life and Casualty promised them, working back at Soup-or-Sub sandwich shop and Quickie Convenience.

Once a month, around Social Security check time, you can find John and Jody Ragsdale, at the Council Bluffs, Iowa casino.

Could lightning strike twice? Hope springs eternal!

Jackpot!

See you soon.

18

"The Centenarian"

H<small>EY</small>! W<small>ANT TO LIVE TO BE A HUNDRED</small>? Ok! Odds are you will! (Well, maybe not if you're already 99.) But be careful what you wish for.

Harold Ramsey turned one hundred years old on November 19, 2037! And he was one miserable human. There was no cake, no candles, no one around to help him celebrate. Not that he even wanted to. He was simply wistful and depressed.

He looked over by the kitchen sink. There was the tomato he'd purchased just 3 days ago. He never touched it, just set it on the counter for later consumption.

It was a gorgeous, smooth-skinned, deep red color when he first set it on the counter, a piece of the vine still connected to its top. But now, it had lost its glow. It was in decay, wrinkled and brown and rotting.

"Just like me," He thought. *"Humans! We're no different than tomatoes."*

He looked down at his aged, thin-skinned hands and creped forearms.

What a cruel joke life plays on those unlucky enough to outlive the rest of the world.

He'd been married (and widowed) twice, fathered three children, all now deceased; had five grandchildren and seven great-grandchildren none of whom ever bothered to call, write, or visit.

Harold had money. Lots of it. He was a saver and had managed things well. The only time he let go of a nickel was to get a better grip! But he didn't know what he'd do with it when he passed. He certainly wasn't giving anything to his estranged grandchildren. He'd probably give it to some worthy charity if there was such a thing.

"I should see somebody about a will I guess."

Harold was lonely. Not just lonely but bored to death! (Pun intended again.) He still lived in the house he bought 50 some years ago, got around ok, and didn't need a cane or walker. He guessed he was in near perfect health. He didn't know for sure, as he hadn't seen a physician in decades.

He had no friends; they had all passed years ago. At times, he laid down the melancholy burden of sanity and considered applying for a job somewhere. Walmart Greeter? Age discrimination?   And, as one might imagine, there aren't many recreational options for the 100-year-old crowd. Golf? With whom? Fishing? Never liked it. No social contacts of any kind since dating sites aren't very productive for people over 100.

So, how much longer would this daily Hell last? Harold was a news junkie and he'd heard time and again about this new United Global 'Death Day Prognosis Project.'

"Would they smirk if I scheduled an appointment? Is it a joke for a centenarian to want to know when the Hell I can get off this planet? It could be this Wednesday!"

The money wasn't a problem. He had plenty of that, and he was sure they'd be happy to take his check. (Old people still write checks.)

"Why not? At least it'll break some of this crazy boredom. Sitting around all day depressed, watching sitcoms."

And so, the next morning, Mr. Ramsey got in his vehicle and programmed it down to the United Global life and Casualty offices, greeted the young lady at the front desk, and made his request to see whomever oversaw *'That Death Day'* thing you people sell!"

"Certainly Sir!"

The young woman pressed a button that summoned a Mr. Thompson from the back of the building, and in moments a middle-aged man appeared with a big, stereotypical insurance agent smile on his face.

"Good afternoon sir! I'm United Global insurance agent Randy Thompson. How can I help you?"

"Well, isn't this the place where you get that 'Death Day' thing?"

'Yessir! It sure is. Why don't you come back to my office and we'll talk about it?"

"I don't need to talk, just tell me how much and let's get going."

The insurance agent could easily see that Harold Ramsey was quite elderly. He wasn't guessing him to be one hundred, but he was certainly no spring chicken. He was somewhat confused but...

"Alright sir, may I ask your name?"

"My name's Harold Ramsey! Now, let's get on with it."

"Yessir Mr. Ramsey. Please come on back and we'll get all the paperwork completed and set up your appointment with the lab-nurse"

Harold was getting irritated.

"Lab Nurse! What the Hell! I just want to know when I'm going to die!"

"Yessir Mr. Ramsey, but we have to give you a full examination before we can ascertain when that will be.",

"Well, damn! Alright, let's get this over with!"

As there were so many individuals who were signing up for the program, they had connected their own, proprietary lab clinic adjacent to the insurance office with a nurse on duty.

Harold grumpily signed all the documents, including the disclaimer, and gave the insurance man his digital coin check for both the Death Day and probable cause. $4200 U.S. The insurance agent wasn't exactly sure what to do with the check. He hadn't ever seen one before.

A quick phone call to the next-door lab and they would see him in 15 minutes. That was fine, Harold literally had nothing else to do.

Once he had divulged his age, everyone, including the nurse was astonished that he was doing this. But he paid for the service, and that is what he would receive.

The procedure was extensive. They drew blood, DNA swabs, checked his vitals and had him fill out questionnaires. This seemed unnecessary to Harold, but they couldn't proceed with things until he acquiesced.

One was a lifestyle questionnaire:

"Do you smoke? Drink alcohol? How much? Do drugs? Etc. etc.

Another was an ancestry questionnaire:

Is your mother living?

"Seriously?"

Father?

It was all so silly, but Harold dutifully gave his blood, peed in a cup, and filled out the questionnaire as required. The entire procedure took about an hour and then they informed him he would get his results in about two weeks.

Ok. Two weeks. But they'd have to mail it. He didn't have the electronic thing-a-ma-jigs to receive the information any other way. The nurse informed him that it wouldn't be a problem.

And so, he headed straight home and the waiting game began. As he opened the door and walked in, the tomato was still there, looking even worse than yesterday if that was possible. It was giving off a pungent odor of decay. He quickly disposed of it.

"Time Flies" is an age-old cliché, and when you're 100 years old, you can surely attest to that. But in those two waiting weeks for his Death Day report, time just dragged on for Harold Ramsey, like a 20-year-old watching the calendar until he'll finally be 21 and legal for all forms of fun.

Then, just as promised, two weeks to the day, there was a knock on the door and a carrier delivered certified mail in a manila envelope. Just as promised, two weeks to the day, his anticipated report arrived.

UNITED GLOBAL LIFE AND CASUALTY

November 30th 2037

Mr. Harold Ramsey
105 Orchard Drive
Medford, Oregon

We, at United Global Life and Casualty, would like to extend our sincere appreciation for your interest in our proprietary actuarial program. We hope this letter finds you well and in good spirits.

I am pleased to report that your completed profile and prognosis is enclosed in this correspondence.

However, to encapsulate the rather lengthy components of the information I have contained within this cover letter the two most important elements. That is, the date and probable cause of your anticipated demise.

- Our empirical actuarial examination of your personal physical profile and other elements, suggests that you will expire on **September 30th, 2042.**

- The probable source for your expiration will be **"Natural Causes due to old age."**

We would like to remind you that, as is enumerated in our disclaimer documents; while our patented actuarial process has been clinically proven to have a high degree of accuracy (98.6%) it is not guaranteed to be one hundred percent precise.

With that, we wish you continued health and happiness for your remaining years.

Sincerely,

Madeline Swathmore

Madeline Swathmore
Vice President/Account Services.
P: 800-727-9800
E: M.Swathmore@UnitedGlobal.com

As he read the cover letter, Harold was incredulous.

"Five years! What the Hell! How can I possibly live five more years?"

This was a dilemma. Something about his life would have to change. How could he live with this incessant boredom and depression for five more years?

Maybe he would travel. Take a cruise. Hang out (If it's possible for centenarians to 'hang out') in the Caribbean or Paris. Maybe he could contact an escort agency and garner a companion. He had all kinds of money and five more good years to go. That's what he'd do.

Soon, he found 'Tiffany,' a twenty-something escort companion who would spend time and travel with him wherever and whenever he'd like for a price. Tiffany would be with him to the very end, and after a time, Harold became so fond of her, that he decided she would be the heir to his fortune.

A few months later, they found themselves renting a villa in the South of France. It was in a quiet little village with magnificent flowering baskets hanging on every light pole and windowsill. Most of the locals got around by bicycle on their narrow, quaint cobblestone streets.

One morning, Harold asked Tiffany if she could please wander out and pick up some groceries from the local market.

She returned about an hour later with a paper bag filled with a freshly baked French baguette, purchased from the petite little bakery just down the block. She also brought cream cheese, eggs bacon, and various other in sundry items.

As she laid them all out on the table, Harold noticed, that off to the side was a smooth, fire engine red, ripe tomato, vine still attached.

Soon, that would put a new wrinkle on things.

19

"You're a Doll!"

Ever heard of synthetic biology? Well, you will. In fact, after you read this book, you'll probably start to notice it all around you. Basically, it's the science of redesigning what already exists in nature. Even back around your time, there were a couple of hundred science labs developing things like synthetic vanilla and such. In fact, in 2016 there were a couple of hundred science labs designing all sorts of synthetics for elements that already occurred. Molecular biology, membrane science, chemical, and biological engineering, and on and on and on.

we only bring this up because up here in 2045 those guys have discovered how to develop synthetic skin. ('Epidermis' if you prefer, we'll get clinical). Already, back in your time, you have realistic, synthetic, anatomically correct, human-like dolls sometimes used as sex toys. Cost: About $6000. But they haven't quite perfected the natural feeling of 'real' skin or made them humanly conversational.

Well, you'll be happy to know that when you get here (and we hope you do); Synthetic Biologists, with the help of artificial intelligence, and mid-twenty-first-century technology have developed Androids with software embedded inside that will converse with you, do your grocery shopping, drive your autonomous vehicle, even have sex with you! Except for their interior manufactured makeup, they are virtually indistinguishable from any human being. Their skin (ok, epidermis) is the same as yours. Looks like it, feels like it, and, frankly, thanks to synthetic biology *is* it. Additionally, these Androids are programmed to appear to have feelings and emotions.

Yep!

And today, in the wondrous world of 2045 America, you can have one of your very own for the exciting *base* price of $75,000 digital bucks plus tax. (C'mon, there's always tax), and some features are optional and cost a bit more. You can customize your order for any age, gender, race, color, or creed. Yes, they'll code the conversational software to Christian, Jew, Muslim, you name it. Every companion is anatomically correct down to the smallest detail, with your choice of short, tall, skinny, fat, big breasts, large penis, clean-shaven, beard, well, you get the idea.

Your own personal Android will arrive in discreet packaging at your doorstep approximately thirty days after ordering.

That brings us to the widowed Janet Powell. Poor Janet lost her husband of 52 years just one year ago. They had never had children, and she was very, very lonely. Janet was 79 years old. She looked younger, but even so, starting a new relationship was almost unthinkable. Money wasn't an issue. Sam had left her well-positioned financially. Janet wondered just how much longer she would have to go through the daily misery of this empty, hollowed out, unfathomable loneliness before her own passing occurred. Surely it wouldn't be much longer. Meanwhile, everyone was talking about this new Global Life and Casualty offering where, for a fee, they will reveal the exact day, month, and year of your last breath.

Back when Sam was still alive, neither one of them wanted to know the answer to that question.

But today, she wasn't so sure. Would she have to live in constant misery for ten or fifteen more years?

Or was her demise right around the corner? That would be just fine with her if there wasn't a lot of pain involved. Life without Sam just had no meaning. Every morning when she woke, it was an unwelcome surprise.

Janet's curiosity about it eventually got the best of her and so she paid the money and took her chances with the United Global Life Prognosis Project. She went in for the lab test and waited just two weeks until the unhappy answer came to her door. Unless she got stung by a killer wasp or attacked by a crazed Chihuahua, Janet Powell was likely to live another 27 years. *"Dammit! Why did she have to take such good care of herself all these years only to be left alone with this melancholy desolation?"*

Janet was going to live to be 106 years old! This was not good. That was nine-thousand-eight-hundred-fifty-five lonely wakeups and melancholy days and nights. Really now, how many games of solitaire can one play? The thought of it was simply unbearable. She began to flirt with the idea of suicide, but her strong Christian religious beliefs prevented any such action.

And then it happened: One afternoon, Janet's casually watching the news and there's a story about those androids we mentioned at the beginning of this chapter.

Bingo!

It was like Divine Intervention! The idea of an 'almost human' Android companion would fill this wretched void in her life! Lonely? Synthetic biology to the rescue.

She would do it! She would contact the company and order him up! Ordering an Android also would assuage the guilt she might feel connecting with another man so soon after Sam's passing. Even though he was gone, she felt a relationship with another man would still be cheating on him. This was different. Now that she had made up her mind to move forward, she had to consider just exactly what she wanted in this companion.

The next morning, she connected on-line with "The Companion Corporation" and was informed that they would send her a Request Menu Form to be filled out designating her preferences for her new associate. She could simply fill it out on-line with their secure server. Once finished, she would simply push the "Submit" button and forward it along with a non-refundable $25,000 digital as the down payment, with the remainder due once the project was completed and approved. She would also be required to 'sign off' her approval at different stages of development.

If, in the interim, she changed her mind about some aspect of her personal companion a 'Change Order' would be issued along with a $1000 'Change Order Fee.'

And so, the process began. She would choose a man six foot two inches tall, height/

weight proportionate and muscular, but not overly so; blue eyes with a full head of hair, just slightly graying, and a well-groomed goatee. His approximate age would be the late sixties and he would speak with a rich, baritone voice. All these attributes came standard. The companion would come with a 125 IQ download. Intelligent Quotients higher or lower would be a $250 per point option, the minimum being 100 and the maximum 160.

Beyond that, there were some personality options. The basic model came with a 'fail safe' conversational congenial demeanor. But, if someone wanted something, shall we say, exotic, one could choose to include as many as six additional voice-activated, interchangeable, personality traits. They would range from the default 'congenial' to 'debate,' 'shy' 'assertive' 'compassionate' 'loving' and 'sad'. These "add-on" software options were $2500 each. For obvious reasons, violent or profane personality traits were strictly prohibited.

After Janet had completed her menu, her total cost added up to $90,000 plus tax. She was perfectly satisfied with most of the *base* characteristics except, she preferred all six optional personality temperaments.

She decided to name him Michael. That name would be programmed into her friend at the factory. Her name (whatever she chose) would also be pre-programmed into his software so he would be addressing her by her name once he arrived and he was 'activated.'

Janet was filled with anticipatory anxiety! Waiting for her companion to arrive was tantamount to a child on Christmas Eve, waiting for Santa to make an appearance while she slept.

And then, after almost six agonizing weeks, there was a knock on the door. Two delivery men stood there with this huge 3' X 5' box and a form that required her signature.

This was it! Michael had arrived. The box appeared to be heavy, and it was. Janet signed the delivery form and opened the door wide for the two men to carry the boxed package inside.

"Where would you like us to set this down Maa'm?"

Janet hadn't given that much thought but instinctively pointed to the living room.

"Would you like us to unpack it for you? That's included in the shipping costs."

She was taken aback by the comment.

"Did the men know what was inside?"

She hoped not.

"No! That's ok! I'll have my son open it later!"

Janet couldn't wait for them to leave. She was filled with excitement. Quickly, she went to the kitchen and grabbed the laser knife. She carefully cut open the box and inside, crouched in a stooped position was her Michael. The instructions inside the box directed her to simply press the small button on the back of the neck to activate, and he would stand up and extract himself out of the box and onto the living room. He looked so real! Then, he immediately began to speak.

"Hello, I'm Michael. I presume you are Janet?"

Janet was momentarily astonished and mes-merized. This was beyond her most fantasized expectations!

Feebly, and with a slight stutter, she answered: *"Uh...uh...yyyes! I'm JJanet!"*

"It is so nice to meet you, Janet! Shall we get acquainted?"

This was surreal.

"Sh...sh...sure! Please have a seat on the sofa We can talk there."

As one might expect, at first, the exchange was awkward for our friend Mrs. Powell, but Michael was a masterful conversationalist, and it wasn't long before she became completely comfortable in the moment, even offering him something to drink, of which he politely declined. He was so real she had forgotten that inside he was all software and circuit boards. There would be no eating or drinking with her new companion.

As time went on, Janet and Michael became inseparable. They would watch the news together and he would assimilate the information the same as she. If he was in 'congenial' temperament mode, they would agree on the perception of politics, crime, or whatever. But when she chose, she would voice activate his "debate" mode and let the games begin.

Janet was in an almost constant state of euphoria. She loved her husband Sam, and for all their married life they got along beautifully. But with Michael, she could control his moods, and have long, interesting conversations about anything she wanted, and he was maintenance-free! She didn't even have to cook for him. In fact, he would cook for her if she asked.

About a month or so into the relationship, she began to consider having him sleep with her. She was apprehensive at first, but it had been so long since having felt the touch of another human. Of course, technically, he wasn't, but that fine line had become so blurred in the relationship, that she never thought about that except at mealtime when she would eat, and he would sit idly by. Finally, one evening, she decided she would activate him into 'loving' mode; and yes, it occurred to her that there might be more to the evening than just cuddling. *(If you know what we mean).*

What's a widowed woman to do? Soon, Michael and Janet were having sex several times a week. It was never advertised or marketed that way by the company, but as it turned out, Janet's companion Michael, was the 2040 version of the Blow-Up Doll. Looks like the widowed Mrs. Janel Powell will be looking forward to twenty-seven years of daily (and nightly) bliss!

But then, as you might expect, there's always some Son- of- a- Bitch who comes along and has to spoil everything.

In this case, it was two Sons- of- Bitches.

They had heard that there was a wealthy widow who lived alone over on the West side of town.

And inside her home was supposed to be a big stash of cash, gold, and diamond jewelry.

To make a long story short, they broke into Janet's house while she was sleeping and came into the bedroom, guns drawn. Michael wasn't asleep, but she had left his temperament in "loving" mode. So, when the burglars came into the bedroom, they were surprised not just to encounter him, but by his welcoming demeanor.

"Hello! I'm Michael! What can I do for you gentlemen?"

His words woke Janet out of deep sleep and what she saw were two, very rough-looking characters with ski masks and laser guns pointed directly at her.

Janet instinctively screamed out loud which caused one of the gunmen to pistol-whip her face while the other had his gun trained on Michael. The pain of the facial attack almost put Janet back to unconsciousness while Michael just sat there in bed, not entirely cognizant of what was going on.

The man who hit her, yelled at her to *"Be quiet!"* She was aghast at his brazen nature and timidly asked; *"What do you want? "What do you want?"*

The man answered with intensity: *"We know you have jewelry and gold here! Just tell us where it is, and we'll leave. Nobody gets hurt!"*

Meanwhile, both men were astonished that Michael was just calmly sitting up in bed.

Somewhat dazed, but still able to think clearly, Janet said: *"Michael! Be assertive!"*

To which Michael exclaimed to the robbers: *"Hey! You guys shouldn't be doing this!"*

Unfortunately, Androids from the Companion Corporation were never programmed for any kind of violence. The harsh language was the best Michael was going to do in this instance.

The burglars couldn't believe what was happening. The lead guy asked her once again,

"Where's the Jewelry Bitch?"

Janet was dumbfounded. And speechless.

He hit her again with the gun. This time making her face swell and bleed.

Michael said again: *"You need to stop this!"*

Finally, in desperation, Janet managed to mumble that there was no jewelry or gold in the house anywhere.

This incensed the man and he hit her one more time across her skull. This knocked her completely unconscious not to be revived.

Then he turned his attention to Michael and demanded he tells them where the jewelry was hidden.

Michael just kept repeating, *"You should not be doing this!"*

With that, the man shot him in the chest. To the surprise of both men, Michael slumped over as if mortally wounded, but there was no blood.

Now, lights were going on all over the neighborhood. People were awakened by the sound of the gunshot. The intruders quickly left the scene of the crime, leaving Janet unconscious and bleeding and Michael slumped over on the bed.

Minutes later, the police arrived. After assessing the situation, they called for the rescue squad ambulance for Mrs. Powell, but were perplexed by this...human?

After weeks in the hospital, the widowed Mrs. Janet Powell was diagnosed with a severe brain injury from which she would never fully recover. Most often, she had no idea where she was or who was present around her.

Where she was, was a rehabilitation center. She would spend the rest of her twenty-seven years there. Slowly degenerating into a permanent coma.

Then again, maybe after the beating she took, she'd get lucky (lucky?) and her 'Death Day'

would come much sooner.

For his part, Michael was shown to be a mixed conglomeration of software and circuitry. He was sent to the trash bin outside the hospital.

Sorry about this sad ending but don't kill the messenger! We just report the facts.

20

"Reincarnation"

As THE SAYING GOES: *"Everybody wants to go to Heaven! Nobody wants to die!"* This was certainly true of a priest friend of ours: Father Dan Kandziolka. Good 'ole Father Dan is one of those guys who knew he wanted to be a Catholic priest from the time he was ten years old. He had an uncle Clement who was a Franciscan Monk and little Daniel just idolized him and wanted to be just like Uncle Clement when he grew up.

And so, he entered the Seminary at a very young age and went through all the rites of passage until, at the young age of 24 he was ordained a Catholic priest forever and ever, amen.

But after almost 3 decades, Father Dan began to wonder how much longer he'd serve The Lord above the grass on planet Earth. More succinctly, Father Dan was beginning to take notice of parishioners of the opposite gender, and occasionally, he was getting that old 'twitch' down in the geographical groin area of his physique. Well, one twitch led to another, and it wasn't long before Father Dan struck up an innocent, platonic counseling relationship with a recently widowed, grieving parishioner. Or, we should say that it was *temporarily* platonic.

Father Dan and the widowed Carolyn Bostic played platonic 'Cat and Mouse' and, as one might expect, eventually found themselves over-stepping the priestly protocol and finding themselves intertwined in a lascivious moment right there in the rectory.

We'll spare you the details, but let's suffice it to say that Father Dan and Carolyn fell in love. With this, Dan was no longer Father Dan but now was part of a couple called Mr. & Mrs. Daniel and Carolyn Kandziolka.

Some good Catholics might say: *"Shame on you Father Kandziolka!"* But then, *"Judge not, lest Ye be judged."*

Being now 56 years of age Daniel became concerned about just how long he would still exist on this planet, enjoying the marital bliss he'd found with Carolyn. The new Mrs. Kandziolka was some twenty years his junior. Her first husband had met an untimely death in an automobile accident. It was likely he would eventually make her a twice-widowed woman, but he was hoping it would be far into the future.

Like just about everyone else, he'd heard of the Actuarial program offered by Global Life and Casualty. By and by, and clandestinely, (no reason to needlessly worry Carolyn), Dan Kandziolka, paid his money, went through the required testing process, and waited to hear about the day of his demise.

In keeping with their timely protocol, Dan received their form letter by certified mail just two weeks later:

UNITED GLOBAL LIFE AND CASUALTY

August 8, 2036

Dear Mr. Kandziolka:

We, at United Global Life and Casualty would like to extend our sincere appreciation for your interest in our proprietary actuarial program. We hope this letter finds you well and in good spirits.

I am pleased to report that your completed profile and prognosis is enclosed in this correspondence.

However, to encapsulate the rather lengthy components of the information contained within this cover letter we would like to point out the two most important elements. That is the date and probable cause of your anticipated demise.

- Our empirical actuarial examination of your personal physical profile and other elements, suggest that you will expire on **December 31st, 2039**
- The probable source for your expiration will be **a 'Cerebrovascular Accident'** more commonly known as **'Stroke.'**

We would like to reiterate that, as is enumerated in our disclaimer documents; while our patented actuarial process has been clinically proven to have a high degree of accuracy (98.6%), it is not guaranteed to be one hundred percent precise.

With that, we wish you continued health and happiness for your remaining years.

Sincerely,

Madeline Swathmore

Madeline Swathmore
Vice President/Account Services.
P: 800-727-9800
E: M.Swathmore@UnitedGlobal.com

Of course, this news was troubling to the newly minted Mr. Kanziolka. If they were right (and there was a high probability, they were) he would be making his exit in just 2 years and 4 months!

Dan was completely taken aback by this prognosis.

"How can this be? I'm healthy as a horse! Why would they predict I'm going to die of a stroke?

He decided not to share the information with Carolyn, though she is the one who signed for the certified package.

She Asked: *"Honey! What was that certified letter you received in the mail about?"*

"Huh? Oh, that was nothing sweetheart! It was from the Church's Insurance Company regarding my Priesthood 401k"

(Well, we call "Bullshit" on that Daniel, but obviously, your wife was fine with that explanation.)

A week later, Dan scheduled a complete physical, MRI, and cat scan with his physician. The radiology report came back showing just 22% artery blockage, which was near perfect for a man his age, and nothing of significance in his brain scan.

This brought considerable relief to Dan. After all, they did indicate that their prognosis wasn't 100% accurate in all cases.

With the optimistic health report, Dan put his worries aside. December 31st, 2036, '37'and '38 went by without a hitch. Dan felt virile and healthy, and his marriage was a model of happiness.

But, as the end of the year 2039 approached, Dan was beginning to get nervous. Really nervous. Out of an abundance of caution, he had a complete physical every single one of the last few years, and they turned out fine.

"Still! What if they were right? What if by some fluke I have this stroke they predicted?"

It was December 30th, 2039. Dan went to his wife and feigned that he wasn't feeling well. In reality, he felt fine physically but his mental state was a wreck. He indicated to Carolyn that he thought perhaps he should go to the hospital. Something was wrong.

For her part, Carolyn became extremely concerned.

"Daniel, Are you alright? Let me see!"

She moved in closer to his face assessing his color. As she pressed her hand to his forehead, she proclaimed. *"Honey, you're skin is clammy and I think you have a fever!*

Clutching his hand over the middle of his torso he said: "I'm having chest pains, Carolyn! Trouble breathing!"

"Oh my God! I'm calling an ambulance!"

"No! No! I'm sure I'll be ok. Let's just have you drive me to the ER, ok?"

"Ok, Babe! But we need to go right now!"

Carolyn drove to the hospital like she was in some kind of race. Dan asked her several times to please slow down but, she was determined to save her husband's life.

Entering the ER there were a dozen people waiting for attention, but chest pain subjects get to go to the front of the line.

They admitted Daniel immediately. First, blood pressure: Slightly elevated, 155/90. Higher than normal, but nowhere near stroke territory. They drew blood as well. No enzymes were detected indicating a heart attack. Mr. Kandziolka's vitals looked fine. Yet, he continued to complain he was suffering chest pains.

In this instance. Despite his vitals being relatively stable. The hospital's not sending him home. Why take the chance of him coding in the parking lot and the litigation that ensues? Besides, admitting him into the hospital overnight is found revenue, and they had plenty of empty Beds on the cardiac floor.

And so, Mr. Daniel Kandziolka was admitted to the hospital just as he'd hoped. His wife came with him to his room and insisted on staying there until he felt better and released.

She would sleep right there with him. Dan was nervous but still, felt fine physically, though he still feigned having chest pains.

All was quiet until 2:14 a.m. December 31st, 2039. Carolyn had fallen asleep in the chair next to Dan's bed. Dan was awake but resting. And, sure as Hell, just as United Global had predicted, a sudden, intense headache had come to visit Dan's cranium. Then, his entire left side went numb. Panic set in. He knew what this was. He tried to speak, wake his wife, but he could not get even one word out, just muffled sounds. Trying to reach for the call button but his arm would not listen to his commands. And then, he collapsed in the bed.

The stroke had begun, and his cardio monitor flat-lined. Dan wasn't dying. He was dead!

Alarm bells went off everywhere. His wife awakened from the chair where she was sleeping. Seeing her husband just lying there Carolyn began screaming in panic. Quickly, they administered the blood clot-busting medicine to open Dan's arteries. It was a race against time. They had no more than 3 minutes to work this out.

No response. Out came the paddles! The EMS guy yelled "Clear!" and Dan jumped up out of the bed. Still no response. They try again! "Clear!" and zap him once more. This time the

EKG flatline started to beep up and down. Dan was back among the living. He'd been gone for almost 2 minutes, but they brought him back.

It seems the 98.6% accuracy rate claimed by United Global Life was a valid claim. Just as prognosticated, Dan Kandziolka died on December 31st, 2039. But because of his cautionary forethought, coming to the hospital, *"just in case"* Dan was saved.

Dan's wife was beside herself.

"Thank God he sensed his chest pains were something serious!"

Carolyn Kandziolka didn't know it was the United Global Prognosis Project that actually predicted it. But hey! Dan was alive. Back from the precipice of the afterlife. And that would suffice. Thank you, Kerry Richmond and company. Score one for the actuarial team.

So, what should Dan Kandziolka do now? Should he share the secret with his wife? Should he go back to United Global and have them re-predict his Death Day once more; or is it better just not to know?

On the other hand, had he not known, he would never have checked into the hospital and probably would have just died at home.

He'd go again. Wonder what they'd say this time?

Bye, Dan!

21

"Who wants to know?"

As THE OLD SAYING GOES: *"Curiosity killed the cat!"* United Global was literally 'minting' money with their proprietary actuarial Prognosis Project. In just a few years since its inception, the revenue from the undertaking had surpassed even that of their insurance business. They had even begun to market 'gift cards'

Still, there were thousands of individuals who *"Would rather not know"* the date of their demise. Our old friend Steve Bastian was one of them. Steve was the president of Bastian Security Systems; a relatively small company (142 employees) that manufactured high-tech security alarms for homes and businesses.

As is a tradition in many companies, at the Christmas party, the employees all 'chipped in' to purchase a special gift for the boss. Guess what the Christmas 2037 bosses' present looked like?

Yep! Congenial boss Mr. Steve Bastian was the proud recipient of a United Global Life and

Casualty Prognosis Project actuarial report gift card!

Steve didn't really want this gift, but it would have been rude and discourteous not to graciously accept it and publicly thank his loyal personnel for their generous offering. This was not an inexpensive gesture. Let's remember, the base price of the United Global actuarial report is $3500.

In any event, as New Year 2038 came around, Mr. Bastian's several subordinates, including his Vice President and even his wife, kept inquiring if he had used his Christmas present yet. This prompted Steve to begin pondering that maybe he should think about going through the process of acquiring his personal report. Initially, he considered just gifting it to a friend or relative who would appreciate it more than he, but he knew it would leak out what he'd done and that would be a big embarrassment and demonstrate an ungrateful attitude towards his workforce.

And so, Mr. Steve Bastian, President of Bastian Security Systems secretly made an appointment with United Global to activate his gift card and take the test. It would take approximately one hour: Medical history, Ancestral and Life-Style Questionnaires, all the usual stuff. He would receive his individualized report in approximately two weeks either by e-mail or certified mail or both. His choice. Steve opted for certified mail only, and now the waiting would begin.

Waiting turned out to be unnerving for Steve. He had not wanted this in the first place, and now his future would arrive on his doorstep in just a few days. Steve wasn't much of a religious sort, but this experiment seemed almost blasphemous. Despite the urgings of his wife and peers, he began to regret he had ever acted on this.

And then, right on time, it arrived. Steve's hand was shaking as he nervously signed for the big Manila envelope. Hands still shaking, he closed the door and stared down at the object. There it was, hidden inside the envelope, the exact day and month and year he would die. He could feel his blood pressure rising as perspiration began to run down his brow. This was too much to absorb. He decided not to open the packet.

Instead, he walked it up the stairs to his home office. and making sure no one was in proximity, he uneasily pushed the combination buttons on his office safe, swung open the door, and inserted the unopened packet inside.

Now, he could tell everyone that "Yes!" he had enacted the process of applying for the

United Global Actuarial project, but that he wanted to keep the information "secret." And that it was, even for Mr. Bastian himself!

Weeks, and then months went by. Most had forgotten about the report, but Steve Bastian thought about it almost every single day. Several times he almost abandoned his discipline and was tempted to open the Devine Declaration of his life's termination, but he resisted.

"Damn! Why did I ever act on this maddening adventure?"

It began to provoke a constant deep depression. One whose cause could not be shared with anyone. Steve's wife noticed it. Her husband, who was almost always a very congenial sort, had become uncharacteristically irritable. His friends and associates at work noticed it as well.

The 2038 Christmas party came and went with barely a word spoken about last year's Christmas gift. People were curious, but the bosses' demeanor was not the same as last year, and it was clear to all that the subject of the Global Life gift was not to be broached; though he again graciously accepted this year's gift which was considerably more modest and appropriate.

New Year's Day, 2039. Our friend Steve Bastian wasn't feeling very well. He didn't know what it was, but something was amiss. His stomach was a little upset, and he had a burning sensation in his left arm.

"All brought on by this incessant stress and depression!" He thought.

He just wasn't himself anymore. Hadn't been for some time. He knew it was all brought on by that Damn report.

"What the Hell! I've had enough! I'm going to open it!"

Cautiously, making sure his wife was nowhere in the vicinity, he got up from the sofa and walked upstairs to his office where the sinister document lie waiting for him in the safe. Punching the numbers, he opened the safe, reached in, and slid the envelope out into his trembling hands.

As he slid the document out of its envelope he began to perspire. His stomach is even more upset than earlier. There, with the United Global Letterhead was his answer:

UNITED GLOBAL LIFE AND CASUALTY

January 12, 2038

Dear Mr. Bastian:

We at United Global Life and Casualty sincerely appreciate your interest in our proprietary Actuarial program. Our empirical process has determined that your expiry will occur on the following date:

January 1st, 2039

While we are cognizant that this date occurs in the relative near future, we must state, as is enumerated in our attached disclaimer documents; that while our patented actuarial process has been clinically proven to have a high degree of accuracy (98.6%), it is not guaranteed to be one hundred percent precise.

Please review the detailed elements included in this report demonstrating the methods by which we arrived at your prognosis.

Accordingly, we would strongly suggest and urge you to seek medical advice as soon as possible as a health professional may be able to thwart the event and prolong your longevity.

Again, we at United Global Life and Casualty appreciate your interest and wish you health and happiness in your enduring times.

Sincerely,

Madeline Swathmore

Madeline Swathmore
Vice President/Account Services.
P: 800-727-9800
E: M.Swathmore@UnitedGlobal.com

Now, panic set in! The pain in his left arm became even more intense. The perspiration soaked his clothing. He felt as though he would regurgitate.

"Oh my God! That's today! I'm going to die today!"

He quickly ran down the stairs, papers in hand, into the kitchen. There was his wife taken aback by his intense appearance. He didn't look good. Steve cried out in a voice filled with panic.

"Judy! I'm dying! I'm going to die today!"

With that, Mr. Steve Bastian collapsed motionless onto the floor, the papers in his hand flying everywhere.

Now, also in a panic, his newly minted widow quickly bent down to come to his aid. Too late! The fifty-six-year-old President of Bastian Security Systems had dropped dead on his kitchen floor.

Irony. If only he had read the actuarial report the day he received it. Anyway, now it was clear why he had changed so much in his last days on this planet.

Meanwhile, things at United Global are getting out of hand.

"Bound to Happen"

YES, THE NICE FOLKS AT UNITED GLOBAL LIFE and Casualty are enjoying another banner year thanks to their patented, proprietary 'Death Day' software. But things aren't all rainbows and unicorns at United Global headquarters.

Allow me to explain: It appears an individual named Kenneth Larsen proffered up his money to see when he might be counted as one of the 'Dearly Departed.' No problem. It was Wednesday, October 19, 2039. Thirty-Five-Hundred Crypto Currency later, the paperwork went in for evaluation and prognosis.

It all landed on the desk of the Actuary, Mike Huckabie. Mike was an experienced, skilled Actuary and his algorithmic calculations were seldom inaccurate. But this time, something went very wrong. After reading the results of his work, he became very concerned. Three times more he re-calculated Mr. Larsen's numbers and every time the outcome was the same.

This situation needed the attention of a Global Executive above his own pay grade.

Accordingly, he gathered Mr. Larsen's documents, quickly walked out into the hallway, pushed the button, and rode the elevator up to the twelfth floor. Once there, he frantically half-walked, half-ran to the corner office which housed Senior Vice President, Roger McMahon, Chief of Underwriting.

Barging in, without announcing his presence, the flustered associate scurried over in front of the now startled executive's desk, documents shaking in his hand.

"Roger! We have a problem! A big problem!"

Roger was awestruck. Mike Huckabie was one of the most even tempered individuals he knew.

This was a Mike he'd never seen before.

"Mike! Calm down! What the Hell is wrong?"

"Listen, Roger! There's this guy who paid to have the prognosis for his 'Death Day!'

"Ok! There are thousands of people like that! What's wrong?"

"He's Dead!"

"What do you mean he's dead?"

"I ran them three times, and the results keep coming up the same. He's dead!"

Roger calmly responded: "Ok! That's the idea. People die! Why is that a problem?"

"It's a problem because he paid for the program on Wednesday, October nineteenth!"

"And?"

"And if the calculations are correct, he died on Monday, November twenty-eighth!"

"And?"

"And today is Thursday, December fifteenth and we haven't delivered the documents yet. He's been dead for almost two weeks!

"Ok! Ok! First, let's find out if he really has passed. Maybe he's still alive! Where's he live?"

"He lives, 'lived' in Fredonia, New York. Roger, this is concerning."

"Alright! The first thing we need to do is check the obits in Fredonia for the last month. If he's listed in there, we'll go to plan 'B'!"

"What's plan 'B'? "

"Plan 'B' is we refund his thirty-five-hundred-dollar processing fee and send a certified letter of condolences to his next of kin apologizing for the delay in administering the results. Then we'll see what happens."

Baffled by Roger's answer, with a befuddled look on his face, Mike Huckabie asked:

"We'll see what happens?"

"Listen Mike, in their grief, they'll probably overlook the delay issue. It's a simple solution. Please calm down!"

He walked out into the hallway once more, this time more sullen than panicked; he took the elevator down to Madeline Swathmore on the fifth floor and presented her with the altered Actuarial letter instructions and a refund acquisition form for Kenneth Larsen

It arrived at the Larsen household on Tuesday, December 20, 2039.

UNITED GLOBAL LIFE AND CASUALTY

December 5, 2039

Dear Ms. Larsen:

   We at United Global Life and Casualty would like to express our sincere condolences for the loss of your spouse, Kenneth.

   As you may be aware, and perhaps in anticipation of his imminent demise, Mr. Larsen had purchased United's proprietary life expiration prognosis program.

   Regrettably, Mr. Larsen had expired while our Actuarial Department Laboratory was in the process of determination of his inquiry.

   Therefore, we have refunded all monies paid by Mr. Larsen for services rendered.   Please review the attached disclaimer documents categorizing our patented and copyrighted actuarial process, while clinically proven to have a high degree of accuracy (98.6%), it is not guaranteed to be 100% percent precise.

   Again, please accept our sincere condolences for your loss.   If you have any questions or comments, please feel free to contact me at your convenience.

Sincerely,

Madeline Swathmore

Madeline Swathmore
Vice President/Account Services.
P: 800-727-9800
E: M.Swathmore@UnitedGlobal.com

Sandra (Mrs. Kenneth) Larsen was well aware that her husband had paid for United's Actuarial process. She was also very cognizant that he had entered the program back in mid-October.

And so, she did, in fact, contact United Global Life and Casualty. But it was through her attorney. Sandra Larsen would be filing a "Wrongful Death" lawsuit against the giant Insurance company for its delay in communicating the results of Mr. Larsen's likely demise.

The lawsuit claimed that had United Global provided the results in a timely manner as stated, their report may have prevented Kenneth Larsen's demise by alerting him to seek medical help from a health professional.

Both Roger McMahon and Mike Huckabie lost their jobs over this mishap.

Let the games begin.

"One Happy Guy!"

JOSEPH STEPANEK JUST COULDN'T stand it anymore. Even though the United Global Life and Casualty Death Prognosis Project had been available to everyone for a few years now, it was still the subject of conversation at the dinner table, water cooler, and snack bar in the country and around the world.

Joseph had several friends who had opted to pay for United Globals' services, and to a person, they were happy with the predicted results. With advances in medical health technology up here in the mid-twenty-first century, most of us will be living long, healthy lives. Wasn't it his turn to acquire his own prognosis?

Joseph's wife was against it. From her perspective, they could spend their hard-earned money a dozen better ways than finding out how and when he was going to die. $4250 digital coin was a big hit for their middle-class income.

Joseph was going to do it anyway. He'd forego the extra $750 for probable cause and, just put out the base $3500. He *did* neglect to tell his wife about it, taking a home equity loan out. He'd have it paid off before she realized he'd done it.

It wasn't long after Joe went through the clandestine process of blood work, questionnaires etc. that the results came back from United Global. And, as we said on the chapter's title page: "Joseph Stepanek was "One Happy Guy!"

In fact, he was sooo happy, that he went right to his wife, admitted to the secret loan he'd taken out, and showed her the *good-news* letter, sent to him by those wonderful folks at United Global Life and Casualty.

He was gonna live! almost forever! They even offered him Life Insurance!

"Here Char! Read the letter!"

UNITED GLOBAL LIFE AND CASUALTY

08/02/2037

Dear Mr. Stepanek:

   After a thorough review of your DNA, blood panel, urinalysis, ancestry, lifestyle questionnaire, and other relevant information, the underwriting department of United Global Life and Casualty has ascertained that barring an Act of God or perishing by your own hand, your last day of life will be:

February 17, 2089.

While we are confident that this date occurs in the distant future, we must state, as is enumerated in our attached disclaimer documents; that while our patented actuarial process has been clinically proven to have a high degree of accuracy (98.6%), it is not guaranteed to be one hundred percent precise.

Please review the detailed elements included in this report demonstrating the methods by which we arrived at your prognosis.

We want to thank you for your patronage of United Global Life and Casualty and, as a gesture of our sincere appreciation, United Global Life and Casualty would like to offer you a discounted whole life insurance policy in any amount you choose.

With your permission, we will contact you in the near future to enquire about your interest in this life insurance proposal.

We at United Global Life and Casualty would like to congratulate you on the anticipated long duration of your future life.

Sincerely,

Madeline Swathmore

Madeline Swathmore
Vice President/Account Services.
P: 800-727-9800
E: M.Swathmore@UnitedGlobal.com

Unless some unforeseen circumstance occurred, Joseph was going to live another fifty-two years. He'd be ninety-eight!

"Maybe we should get your prognosis Honey! I'm sure we'll grow old together!"

Joe's wife, Charlene, while happy to hear the news of her husband's longevity, was still not overjoyed at the prospect of a $3500 home equity loan.

"Joe! I'm happy for you, and us; but we can't afford another $3500, and I'm sure I'll be with you till the end. Anyway, I don't really want to know!"

Still, at this point, the money was, 'water under the bridge,' and she decided to celebrate with him. For his part, Joe purchased a 30-year term, $1 million dollar life insurance policy at a deeply discounted rate. No medical exam was required, as he'd already entered Global's actuarial project. As far as they were concerned, he would out-live his policy.

In a week or so, the dust had settled, and life went almost back to normal. But, a few months later, Joseph was experiencing pain in his hands and feet that wouldn't go away. He considered it must be arthritis or some such condition.

Joseph was an avid golfer. He would golf in virtually any weather except in snow or extremely low temperatures. But this summer, he noticed he didn't perspire no matter how hot things got out on the course. Also, there were dark red spots suddenly appearing between his belly button and upper thighs. *"Heat Rash?"* Finally, a wheezing cough was coming on more regularly than he'd appreciate. Plus, the embedded computer chip in his arm was sending a health warning signal to his physician that his kidneys weren't working at optimal levels.

After the alert, his doctor's office notified him of a request to make an appointment at his earliest convenience to determine just what was going on.

In a thorough examination, including MRIs, X-rays, Body Scans, blood tests, etc. no abnormalities were found except for a malfunction in Joseph's kidneys brought on by an unknown cause. The doctor prescribed "Farixiga", a drug therapy developed in the mid-2020s that would effectively treat his kidney problem. They attributed the dark red spots on his abdomen as 'Heat Rash' and sent him on his way with assurances this 'kidney' thing would improve in time.

Three months later, Joseph Stepanek was dead. He died of an extremely rare disorder, called Farber Disease. Acquired by less than 1/1,000,000 people, it is almost always fatal, even with early diagnosis. (You think we'd make this disease up? Google it!)

Because of its rarity, neither United Global nor Joseph's physician was able to accurately diagnose the condition. And so, Mr. Joseph Stepanek became one of the 1.4% sad erroneous statistics of the 98.6% accuracy of United Global Life and Casualty's Death Day Prognosis.

Charlene Stepanek, wept uncontrollably at her husband's funeral and wept even more intensely when the $1 million dollar life insurance check was hand-delivered to her door.

And so, life goes on. (But not for Joseph Stepanek).

"Capital Punishment"

CARLOS AND MARIA MORALES were a handsome, middle-aged couple who had migrated as children from Guatemala to America during the Biden Administration.

They grew up together in South Texas, fell in love, got married, got their citizenship, had two beautiful children, and worked, as they say, their *"Fingers to the Bone"* in the cotton fields of Texas and saved and saved and saved until finally, they could buy their own home.

It wasn't any kind of a mansion. We might call it a 'starter' home; maybe even a bungalow, but still, it was theirs. They marveled at their incredible luck to purchase the house at a greatly discounted price to other, comparable dwellings in the neighborhood. For some reason, not revealed to the Morales' the previous owners were very motivated to sell.

But not long after they moved themselves in, it was beginning to become clear just what the motivation was: Mr. and Mrs. Schmidt and family were the neighbors seemingly spawned from Hell. At all hours of the day and night, you could sometimes hear glass crashing through the open windows and the father screaming profanities at the wife and kids.

Like most Latinos, the Morales family were very religious, church-going Catholics. The language emanating from the house next door would make a drunken sailor blush. To make matters worse, there were empty beer bottles and half-broken, tipped-over lawn chairs and such, strewn all over the seldom mowed front yard. These were not refined people.

For the most part, the Morales' kept to themselves, and after a few months, they began to adapt themselves and tried to block out the constant noise and chaos manufactured by their new neighbors.

Occasionally, both Mr. Schmidt and one or more of the Morales family would be out front at the same time, but Karl Schmidt never bothered to introduce himself or even wave *"hello!"* Carlos thought it wise not to be the one to instigate an introduction, but to just go about whatever outside chore he was doing and stay away.

Karl Schmidt was clearly what most of us would call a die-hard, 'White Supremacist Red Neck,' Sometimes he'd just sit out on his front steps dragging on a marijuana joint and washing the smoke down with a can of Budweiser. One could see from the scant t-shirts he wore while sitting there that he was completely tattooed from the waist up to his neck and though it couldn't be revealed through his dirty worn jeans, one could be pretty sure he had tats all the way down to his toes.

It might take a while, but something bad was eventually bound to happen between the two neighbors. And, one Sunday morning as the Morales' were driving home from Church, the predicable event began to unfold.

To put it simply, as the Morales family was pulling into their humble driveway, they observed Karl Schmidt beating the living Hell out of his wife with his belt, right out on the front lawn. Inside their vehicle, the Morales' were all frozen with fear. Fear for Karl Schmidt's wife and fear that the violence might spill over into their yard.

Should Carlos run over and try to stop his neighbor before he kills his wife? Carlos wasn't a coward, but he wasn't a fighter either. Plus, standing only five feet five inches tall he'd be no match for the hulking, infuriated monstrous beast.

Also, looking around, he could see no one else in the neighborhood were outside their homes.

Obviously, all the neighbors were used to this kind of thing and stayed locked up tight inside.

Fortunately, after a continued minute or so of screaming profanities and drawing blood from his wife's face, it all ended as he grabbed her by her hair, opened the half-broken screen door, and literally threw her inside the house.

Once inside their own home, Maria and Carlos decided their neighbor's wife might be in mortal danger. There was still screaming going on inside the Schmidt household but, this time they were terrified screams obviously emanating from the wife.

They decided to call the police. This was not a good idea.

Thirty minutes later, a police cruiser pulled up on the Schmidt's driveway. They'd been here before. Knocking delicately on the flimsy front door, they were soon confronted by a snarling, tattooed, goliath demon.

Peering at the two officers through the half-ripped-up screen, Karl Schmidt bellowed:

"Yeah! What the Hell do you two want?"

"Sir, we received a call about a domestic disturbance at this household. We're here to investigate."

"Well, there ain't no domestic disturbance going on here so you two can just get the Hell off my property!"

"Sir, may we come in for just a minute and see if everything's alright? If it all checks out, we'll leave!"

Karl Schmidt scowled: *"Yeah, just a second, I'll get my wife. Be right back."*

Karl came back alright. But not with his wife. Instead, he brought a Colt Python, 357 magnum pistol, and before the cops could react, he blew them both off his cement porch and onto the ground below

Still enraged, and quite sure that it was his neighbor who called the police, he walked briskly over to the Morales household, kicked in the front door, walked into the living room where Carlos and Maria were sitting, and shot both of them dead as well. Luckily, the children were in their room and escaped the terror.

Of course, it was an 'open and shut case of cold-blooded murders and Mr. Schmidt was summarily convicted and sentenced to death.

"Mr. Schmidt with the power invested in me by the great State of Texas, I hereby sentence you to death in the electric chair. Your execution will take place at 1:30 a.m. on the 24th of June 2039."

Curiously, Karl Schmidt's reaction was to laugh uncontrollably as the judge pronounced the sentence. As the bailiffs led him away from the courthouse, he continued to laugh maniacally!

By law, every individual convicted of Capital murder is entitled to appeal before execution. But Karl Schmidt had no interest in appealing his sentence. His own attorneys were perplexed by his stubborn refusal.

Some months later, everyone discovered the reason for Mr. Schmidt's adamant response. As the prison guard came to his cell for the nightly roll call, Karl Schmidt did not respond. As he looked into the cell, he saw Karl lying on the floor motionless.

Calling for backup and opening the cell door, there was the lifeless, body of Death Row Inmate, Karl Schmidt. Lying next to him were some paper documents with the header, "United Global Life and Casualty"

UNITED GLOBAL LIFE AND CASUALTY

08/02/2036

Dear Mr. Schmidt:

After a thorough review of your DNA, blood panel, urinalysis, ancestry, lifestyle questionnaire, and other relevant information, the underwriting department of United Global Life and Casualty has ascertained that barring an Act of God or perishing by your own hand, your last day of life will be:

May 30th 2039

While we are confident that our prognosis occurs in the relatively near future, we must state, as is enumerated in our attached disclaimer documents; that while our patented actuarial process has been clinically proven to have a high degree of accuracy (98.6%), it is not guaranteed to be one hundred percent precise.

Please review the detailed elements included in this report demonstrating the methods by which we arrived at your prognosis.

We want to thank you for your patronage of United Global Life and Casualty

Sincerely,

Madeline Swathmore

Madeline Swathmore
Vice President/Account Services.
P: 800-727-9800
E: M.Swathmore@UnitedGlobal.com

Well, stated or not, once again United Global Life and Casualty hit the dated bullseye.

It seems Inmate Karl Schmidt had beaten the system.

But at least Mrs. Schmidt would not be beaten again.

See you soon.

"The Gambler"

As THE OLD SAYING GOES: *"Casinos don't build those multi-million dollar elaborate buildings with upscale restaurants and opulent interiors by paying out winners!"* Even a 'first-time' gambler is aware that the 'House' has a distinct advantage when they wager a bet. Whether it's on a slot machine or a blackjack table, the 'House' oversees the advantage.

The same applies to Insurance Companies. In fact, any Casino operator would kill to have the odds advantage enjoyed by life insurance companies. When you buy a term life insurance policy, there is just a 1% chance that anyone will ever collect on that policy. 99% of term life insurance policies expire worthless. Perhaps, instead of being called *United Global Life and Casualty*, its name should be changed to *United Global Life and Casino*! Basically, when you purchase a term life insurance policy, the chances are 'slim and none' that your beneficiary will ever receive the funds. Of course, the

Insurance Companies know this, and that's why term insurance policies are so inexpensive.

And so, we begin the story of Gregory Sabatka. Back in the year 2012, 53- year-old Mr. Sabatka purchased a $1 million, 20-year term life insurance policy from our good friends at United Global Life and Casualty.

Gregory Sabatka came from a very large, West Virginia coal-mining family. In fact, he enjoyed the company of 16 uncles and aunts and 65 first cousins. Most of his aunts were still alive but, his father, grandfathers, and virtually all his uncles except one had died in their 50s. Though Mr. Sabatka did not endure the rigors of the coal mines as did his elders and ancestors, he was quite sure that genetics would dictate that, he too, would die somewhere in his 50s or close by.

If you strip away all the formalities, one Gregory Sabatka was placing *a bet* ($4000 annual insurance premium) that he would die before the next 20 years expired. United Global Life and Casualty happily took the other side of that *bet*, because, even back in the year 2012, before anyone had heard or even thought of the Actuarial 'Death Day Prognosis Project,' United Globals' actuarial processes were very, very good. They were quite sure Mr. Sabatka would out-live his policy for which they would collect a total of $80,000 until the year 2032 when the policy would expire worthless. Take that kind of money from a couple of hundred thousand individuals and you can see how they build those mammoth buildings that house the Insurance Company's headquarter operations.

We're sure you can guess what happened. It's 2032 and the very much alive, 73-year-old Gregory Sabatka was, of course, one of the 99% statistics. By 2032 he had wagered and lost $80,000 with United Global Life and Casino, and was, what is known in the industry as 'Insurance Poor!' He had none.

For Gregory, the good news was he didn't die; and the bad news was he didn't die. Though he was happy to not have expired, Gregory was still concerned that he had no life insurance to protect his family.

And then, in 2035, along came the United Global Life and Casualty "Actuarial Death Day Prognosis Project" For $3500 digital he could ascertain the exact day he would expire. If it were long into the future, he could again purchase life insurance (this time 'Whole Life' which never expires), and problem solved.

Though he wasn't wealthy, Gregory Sabatka was not without means. He decided to purchase the Actuarial Prognosis from United Global. He was sure he was still in good health and when the report came back validating that to be true, he would use the validation to purchase insurance again, but this time with another insurance company. Justified or not, Gregory had animus toward United Global and would not be providing them with even more wasteless life insurance premiums. Two weeks later, his personal report came back, and it was just as he expected.

UNITED GLOBAL LIFE AND CASUALTY

04/16/2036

Dear Mr. Sabatka:

After a thorough review of your DNA, blood panel, urinalysis, ancestry, lifestyle questionnaire, and other relevant information, the underwriting department of United Global Life and Casualty has ascertained that barring an Act of God or perishing by your own hand, your last day of life will be:

February 7th, 2057

While we are confident that our prognosis provides you with many more years of good health we must state, as is enumerated in our attached disclaimer documents; that while our patented actuarial process has been clinically proven to have a high degree of accuracy (98.6%), it is not guaranteed to be one hundred percent precise.

Please review the detailed elements included in this report demonstrating the methods by which we arrived at your prognosis.

We want to thank you for your patronage of United Global Life and Casualty

Sincerely,

Madeline Swathmore

Madeline Swathmore
Vice President/Account Services.
P: 800-727-9800
E: M.Swathmore@UnitedGlobal.com

The United Global letter was incredibly good news for Gregory Sabatka. He would be 97 years of age before he expired. Hallelujah!

Gregory immediately contacted the Coronado Life Insurance Company and applied for yet another $1 million-dollar 20-year term policy. Since the predicted end to his life on this planet was in the far future, Gregory changed his mind regarding the 'Whole Life' policy. He surmised that, if accepted, he could again pay the much smaller premiums of a term policy rather than the more expensive 'Whole Life.'

And so, after Coronado's required medical exam process along with the United Global Actuarial Prognosis report, Gregory Sabatka was once more insured to the tune of $1 million U.S. dollars.

Gregory Sabatka was elated. He could now look forward to continued long life and, in the meantime, his survivors were protected in the event he would experience an unforeseen (and now untimely) demise.

Meanwhile, Gregory's wife Katie purchased her own United Global Actuarial Report and was prognosticated to live some three years longer than himself. The good news just kept on coming. Their lifelong dream was to live in Italy, Retirement was way overdue for both, and the longevity prediction from United Global, coupled with a nice savings stash said: "Let's do it!"

Katie and Gregory sold their home in West Virginia, kissed the kids goodbye, and sailed away to live in a small, quaint Italian village north of Naples.

For years, life was good for Katie and Greg. Italy was all they had dreamed it would be. But, early in his 79th year, Gregory began experiencing heaviness in his chest. Sure, that he would live at least another 18 years he ignored the cautionary signals the health chip embedded in his arm was sending and never shared the experience with his wife.

And then it happened. One late evening, while lying in his bed asleep. Gregory Sabatka's life came to an abrupt ending. His wife awakened to find him motionless and unresponsive. It appeared the 1.6% error rate of the United Global Actuarial Prognosis had come to fruition yet again. Where's Kerry Richmond when you need him?

"How could this be? He was destined to live almost forever!"

Following the shock and unbearable grief, his wife experienced; funeral arrangements were made, and Gregory's body was flown to the

U.S. for burial.   Subsequently, Katie Sabatka filed an insurance claim with the Coronado Life Insurance Company.

Claim Denied!

CORONADO LIFE INSURANCE COMPANY

2283 Coronado Way, Seattle, Washington

April 27, 2041

Dear Mrs. Sabatka:

We are in receipt of your claim of life insurance settlement in the case of the demise of your spouse, Mr. Gregory Sabatka.

It is with deep regret that we are unable to honor your foreign death claim at this time as we are required to further investigate the proof and manner of Mr. Sabatka's demise outside of the United States.

In accordance with our insurance contractual agreement, it was required that Mr. Sabatka inform Coronado Insurance of his foreign destination, the length of time he intended to reside, and what activities he will engage in while there.

Additionally, customary practices, resources, and technology all vary greatly from country to country, which precludes Italy from recording a death in the same way that is practiced here in the United States. Therefore, a Foreign Death Certificate may not adhere to the requirements of proof of death in the United States.

We at Coronado Life Insurance would like to extend our sincere condolences for the loss of your spouse, Gregory Sabatka.

Yours Truly,

Samuel Johnson

Samuel Johnson
Senior Vice President,
Account Services
Coronado Life Insurance Company

Well, there you go. It appears there are lots of reasons term life insurance policies don't pay. Many, and maybe most, insurance companies find ways to deny death claims. One that is common in almost all life policies is the 'Foreign Death Claim' clause. Even up here in 2045.

When insurance companies are given foreign 'proofs-of-death' or death certificates that look unusual compared to the U.S.'s death recording practices, they often allege they are being victimized by people faking their deaths and will launch their own investigations. Who knew?

Read that fine print folks!

26

"Yule Died Greetings!"

PROBABLY NOBODY ON PLANET EARTH enjoyed Christmas more than Clarice Colway. At the tender age of eight years, she learned the sad truth about the Easter Bunny, Tooth Fairy, and Santa Claus. And while the Easter Bunny and Tooth Fairy were easy concepts to abandon, the Santa Claus thing came with somewhat more difficulty.

"Surely there's a Santa Claus. He comes to my house every year! He eats the cookies I leave on the fireplace mantle! How can this be?

Despite her parental guidance, Clarice continued her belief in the jolly old elf well into her early teens, until the entire idea became untenable, and puberty replaced her childhood fantasies.

But Christmas was still at the top of her holidays. It was truly "The most wonderful time of the year." Decorating the tree, gift-giving, Christmas dinner, Christmas Carols, the whole atmosphere was always magical. Every year, as Thanksgiving approached, Clarice became ebullient. Christmas was almost here!

It was September, but Christmas was always on her mind. One sunny, balmy fall morning while relaxing on the front porch, the now 87-year-old Clarice began to contemplate just how many more Christmas' she would enjoy. These days, people, and especially women, lived to be well into their 90s and beyond.

For some time, she had been aware of the United Global Life and Casualty, Life Prognosis Project. She had long ago decided not to participate, choosing not to know when the last Christmas of her life would occur. But now, just as millions of others had succumbed to the curious temptation to know, it had become obvious to her that she had way more yesterdays than tomorrows, she considered, she would join the crowd and just see how many more tinsel holidays were ahead. She would extract $3500 from her more than ample bank account and enter the fray.

She got up from her porch rocker, went inside and called the local United Global agent office, and set up the appointment. They scheduled her for the very next day at 10 a.m. and an hour later her document package was shipped off to United Global headquarters.

Just as promised, the results came back exactly 14 days later.

UNITED GLOBAL LIFE AND CASUALTY

10/19/2041

Dear Ms. Colway:

After a thorough review of your DNA, blood panel, urinalysis, ancestry, lifestyle questionnaire, and other relevant information, the underwriting department of United Global Life and Casualty has ascertained that barring an Act of God or perishing by your own hand, your last day of life will be:

December 25th, 2041

We recognize that the date we have ascertained is in the very near future and we would strongly encourage you to confer with your attending physician as soon as possible. They may have solutions that could possibly extend your survival.

While we are confident that our prognosis provides you with an accurate life expectancy, it is important to note that, as is enumerated in our attached disclaimer documents; our patented actuarial process has been clinically proven to have a high degree of accuracy (98.6%), it is not guaranteed to be one hundred percent precise.

Please review the detailed elements included in this report demonstrating the methods by which we arrived at your prognosis.

We want to thank you for your patronage of United Global Life and Casualty

Sincerely,

Madeline Swathmore

Madeline Swathmore
Vice President/Account Services.
P: 800-727-9800
E: M.Swathmore@UnitedGlobal.com

"What! I'm going to die this Christmas! How can this be? Dying on her favorite day in all the world AND this year!"

Clarice was beyond incredulous. Surely, a mistake. She felt fine. The medical chip embedded in her arm was giving no alerts. She quickly dialed up her primary physician's office via Tele-Med and hooked her 'med-chip' up to the analysis machine. There was one small blip showing her blood sugars were off just a bit, but other than that, all her vitals appeared normal. She didn't divulge her United Global experience to her doctor, and he assured her that she was in excellent physical condition.

Now she was non-plussed. Unsure of what she should do. Should she believe the doctor or the insurance company? If they were right, she had just a couple more months to live, and to die on Christmas day would be the ultimate irony.

Still, Clarice had always been a bit of a hypochondriac, and even though she was given assurances that all was well, she was also aware that the United Global life Prognosis Project was known to be very accurate. thousands of cases had been reported to the media as 'right on,' why should hers be different?

Just as she had done for all her adult life, Clarice went through the motions and traditions of the holidays. Wrapping presents, trimming the tree, sending cards to friends and relatives, never mentioning the United Global prognostication.

Christmas Eve was, without a doubt, the longest day of Clarice's life. Would she be dead tomorrow? She was supposed to go to her daughter's house for Christmas dinner with the whole family. What if she never woke up? What if she dropped dead at the dinner table?

Sleeping was out of the question. She would be awake (or dead) at midnight on Christmas Day.

But midnight came and went and by 2 a.m., she could no longer keep her eyes open. Clarice Colway went to sleep unsure if she would ever wake up to see the light of day.

When it came, she was still there. Awakened by her phone. It was her daughter:

"Merry Christmas mom! Just checking to see if you're ok! Remember, Christmas dinner is at 3 p.m."

"Ok Honey! I'll be there. I'm excited to see all the grandchildren!"

And so, it went. Would Clarice die at dinner? On the drive over? In bed at night? It was all so disconcerting. She had always loved Christmas festivities, but this year was very different.

Dinner went well. Her grandchildren fawned all over her and after dinner, everyone gathered around the tree and opened their gifts and laughed and loved and enjoyed the entire experience. But Clarice had this 'thing' hanging over her and her daughter could sense something was awry.

"Mom! Are you ok? You feeling, ok?"

This certainly wasn't the time to be going to confession.

"Huh? Oh yes, honey, everything's perfect. Thank you so much for the beautiful wrap. I just love it!"

Accordingly, the evening ended around 7 p.m. with hugs and kisses and *"I love you"* all around. Eventually, Clarice made it to her vehicle for the short 15-minute drive home. Would she die in her sleep tonight? She was too tired from last night's fiasco to stay awake much longer.

10:16 a.m. Thursday, December 26th. Clarice Colway awakens to sunlight on her face through the half-drawn curtains in her bedroom. She's alive. Perfectly alive and well-rested and...

"What the Hell is going on here? Well, I guess it's good news. I'm obviously not dead; in fact, I'm feeling pretty damn good!"

Weeks go by. Clarice is still hesitant and nervous about the prediction of her ending, but she's waking up every morning feeling chipper. And then comes a knock on the door. There stands the mail carrier with a certified envelope requiring her signature.

"What's this?"

The return address was United Global Life and Casualty. Frantically, Clarice opened the envelope to read its contents.

UNITED GLOBAL LIFE AND CASUALTY

01/14/2042

Dear Ms. Colway:

We hope this letter finds you in good health.

We are writing today to inform you that after a review of your Actuarial prognosis, we have discovered a clerical error in our previous report. Previously, we reported to you that the date of your demise would be December 25th, 2041, of last year. In fact, the prognosis date should have read:

December 25th, 2047

We want to extend our most sincere apologies for this egregious clerical error, and it is our hope that it did not cause you undue consternation during the holiday season.

Generally, we are confident that our prognosis provides you with an accurate life expectancy, however, mistakes are sometimes made, which is why we review all prognosis reports for accuracy, even after they are reported to our valued clients. Additionally, it is important to reiterate that, as is enumerated in our attached disclaimer documents; while our patented actuarial process has been clinically proven to have a high degree of accuracy (98.6%), it is not guaranteed to be one hundred percent precise.

Again, please accept our sincere regret for our inaccurate reporting of the prognosis of your imminent demise. We want to thank you for your patronage of United Global Life and Casualty

Sincerely,

Madeline Swathmore

Madeline Swathmore
Vice President/Account Services.
P: 800-727-9800
E: M.Swathmore@UnitedGlobal.com

While there was some relief in the transcript from United Global, there was also a sense of rage that came upon her. She would seek legal counsel and inquire about filing a suit.

However, after consultation with a 'Personal Injury' attorney, it was clear that the disclaimer addendum attached to her initial report provided 'air-tight' indemnification for United Global Life and Casualty. Obviously, their army of attorneys had thought of every possible litigious circumstance long before the program was put into place.

Happy Holidaze! LOL

27

"Love you to death!"

ROBERT COCHRAN WAS MARRIED for 23 years. Robert really loved MaryAnn. Unfortunately, MaryAnn wasn't Robert's wife. Her name was Samantha, and he really didn't love her anymore. As we said, he really loved MaryAnn.

By now, we're quite sure you've figured out that Robert and MaryAnn were having an affair. MaryAnn loved Robert too. She wasn't married, so the only problem was the one in the middle of this torrid love affair named "Samantha"

What to do, what to do? Well, the obvious answer was for Robert to divorce Samantha, but like so many other conniving husbands, that just wouldn't do for Mr. Cochran. Samantha had been diagnosed with Parkinson's three years earlier and they had three beautiful children together and a grandchild on the way. Not to mention 23 years of marital bliss (or, whatever you call it before MaryAnn stepped in.) He'd have to find another way to be with his new soul mate.

This affair had been going on for almost 2 years and MaryAnn was losing her sense of humor about Robert being still married. She would ask woefully:

"Do you love me, Robert? Do you really love me?"

With a tinge of indignation, he would reply:

"Of course, I love you! You know that!"

"Then divorce her and marry me!"

Now, slightly irritated by her bold suggestion he said:

"It's not that easy, and you know it!"

Maryann was becoming despairing. With her hands solidly cemented on her hips, she commented with scathing sarcasm:

"So, we just go on like this forever, renting hotel rooms, sneaking all around town?"

"Of course not!"

"Well, what then?"

Pursing his lips, with obvious aggravation, Robert said:

"I'll take care of it ok?"

MaryAnn rolled her eyes. She'd heard that from him dozens of times before. It was the same old put-off.

"Take care of it how? What are you going to do? When?"

Her incessant prodding was making him even more irritated:

Don't worry about it, I said I'll take care of it!"

Robert had begun to think the unthinkable. He didn't have the character or courage to just go home and announce: *"I'm leaving you!"* She would be devastated beyond all reason. To date, even though this affair had been ongoing for almost two years, Samantha hadn't the slightest suspicion.

He had become so deeply in love with MaryAnn, that he would do whatever it took to escape his marriage and be with her. MaryAnn had already given him an ultimatum, he knew, he had better do something soon or risk losing her forever.

Other than divorce or legal separation, there was only one other real option, and that was the 'unthinkable' part. Robert would have to 'eliminate' Samantha. He wasn't a criminal. How could he do that? Was he that much in love? Would he even do that to be with MaryAnn?

"Am I willing to do this? Am I really considering that? Am I crazy? Murder my wife? My God! What have I become? This isn't me! (Oh! But yes, it is Robert. Shame on you!)

It's interesting that throughout history, rather than divorce their spouse, time after time, case after case. many individuals have decided to end the lives of their significant other. They sometimes got caught and sometimes not.

Meanwhile, when we would read or hear about someone caught in the act, most of us ask:

"Why didn't he just divorce her?"

Well, as I explained above, divorce just wasn't going to work for our friend Robert Cochran, so he would have to kill his beloved. But how to do it? When to do it? He was on the clock with MaryAnn's impatience. They say there's no such thing as the perfect murder. However:

An accidental fall down the basement steps onto the hard cement floor seemed the most likely strategy for someone who wasn't a professional assassin. The fact that Samantha had been stricken with Parkinson's would help some. Her balance was impaired and when she walked, she was very unstable. An accident of that type would be very plausible.

And so came the weekend. Just the two of them in the house. Samantha was on the living room sofa taking a nap. Robert was supposedly watching football in the adjoining room. Gathering all his composure, Robert rose and went to the basement door. Nervously, he called out to his wife:

"Sam! Come look at this would you?"

Samantha, cocked her head up. Did she hear something? She hollered out:

"Bob! Did you just call for me?"

"Yes Honey! Down here in the cellar! Something's wrong! I think an animal might have crawled in through a basement window!"

With that, Samantha Cochran hobbled around the stairs to the open basement door where Robert was standing. He moved her in front of him at the edge of the stairs and cried:

"Look!"

And then he shoved her headfirst down into the basement. Samantha let out a short scream as she tumbled down the twelve wooden steps to the floor, her head bouncing off the cement at the bottom. Bob yelled: *"Oh my God!"* half in disbelief with what he had done. He quickly scurried down to check and see. Samantha was motionless but still breathing. She had not yet succumbed to the blows of the fall.

No time to back out now! Robert picked his wife up by her head and banged it intensely several times on the cement floor. Samantha gave out a big sigh. Unconscious, but still breathing. And so, he repeated the same ritual. That did it.

Immediately, as he had planned, Robert called 911:

"This is 911, what is your emergency?"

"Oh my God! Oh my God! My wife has fallen down the stairs and she's unconscious! Please

come now! Oh my God!" (Geesh! How many Gods does this guy have?)

"Please try to be calm sir! What is your address?"

We're sure you can guess the rest. The paramedics showed up shortly thereafter and found Mrs. Cochran lying dead on the now blood-splattered cellar floor.

Mr. Cochran wasn't an actor but, he certainly gave an academy award-winning performance of a man in grief for the attending crew. After he gave them his statement and she was carried away to the morgue, Robert called MaryAnn.

"Hello?"

"Sweetheart, it's me!"

"I know! What's wrong?"

"Well, something terrible has happened. Samantha fell down the basement stairs tonight and hit her head on the floor! She's dead MaryAnn! She's dead!"

Shocked at the news, MaryAnn leaned back and gawked at the phone speaker embedded in her arm. Was he joking?

"Oh my God! She's dead?"

On the chance the conversation was somehow being recorded, Robert feigned a voice of distress and astonishment:

"Yes! I don't know what to do!"

MaryAnn knew what this meant. She too feigned sympathy for Robert, but of course, this was her dream come true.

"Do you want me to come to you, Babe?"

"No! No! I have to call the kids and tell them what happened! I'll come to see you after I'm through."

"Ok, please come to me as soon as you can. I'm so sorry Robert."

Of course, MaryAnn wasn't any kind of sorry. Now Robert would be hers for all eternity.

A week went by. The Morgue had not yet released Samantha's body, pending an autopsy, so the funeral would be delayed. The children were grief-stricken themselves and tried very hard to comfort their father but, it seemed to no avail.

It was time to clean out the remnants of Samantha's presence in the house. Robert went upstairs to their bedroom and open the drawers to her dresser. In the second drawer, underneath her underthings was a large, manila envelope. The return address was from United Global Life and Casualty. An insurance policy? Robert pulled out the contents. The first page was a cover letter.

UNITED GLOBAL LIFE AND CASUALTY

10/10/2041

Dear Ms. Cochran:

    It is with sincere regret that we are writing you today to inform you of the prognosis for your report. Due to the severity of your Parkinson's Disease, our Actuarial Department has ascertained the exact date of your demise will be.

November 14, 2041

Because this date is imminent, we strongly urge you to seek medical advice regarding your condition as, perhaps, health professionals may be able to prolong your longevity.

Additionally, while we are confident that our prognosis provides you with an accurate life expectancy, mistakes are sometimes made and it is important to note that, as is enumerated in our attached disclaimer documents; while our patented actuarial process has been clinically proven to have a high degree of accuracy (98.6%), it is not guaranteed to be one hundred percent precise.

Please review the detailed elements included in this report demonstrating the methods by which we arrived at your prognosis.

Again, please accept our sincere regret for our prognosis of your imminent demise. We want to thank you for your patronage of United Global Life and Casualty

Sincerely,

Madeline Swathmore

Madeline Swathmore
Vice President/Account Services.
P: 800-727-9800
E: M.Swathmore@UnitedGlobal.com

Robert could not believe what he was reading. Apparently, Samantha had submitted herself to the United Global Actuarial Prognosis Project without his knowledge. If the prognosis was correct, Samantha would have died of natural causes in the next five days.

Robert Cochran murdered his wife needlessly! He sat down on the bed and began to sob uncontrollably. He was a murderer! He murdered his terminally ill wife. She loved him too much to divulge what she already knew.

Just then, there was a knock on the door. Robert wiped his eyes and came downstairs to see who was knocking. Through the glass, he saw two, well-dressed men who flashed police detective badges.

"Police Detectives! What could they possibly want?"

28

"Super Star!"

As you're probably aware, the greatest of all time (GOAT) football Quarterback in your day was a guy named Tom Brady. But up here in the 2040s Sean Callahan was the man! He broke any, and all records. Played until almost 50 years of age and guided the Oklahoma Oilers to 8 Super Bowl victories and was voted MVP every single time.

Like many others, Sean Callahan was drawn to the United Global Prognosis Project. While there were still thousands of 'holdouts' who really didn't want to know their 'Death Day,' Mr. Callahan was curious as Hell.

During the 2043 season, he decided he would visit the local United Global agent's office and begin the process of blood work and questionnaires to see when his day would come.

Sean wasn't at all concerned. He was sure he had decades of life to live far into the future.

After all, the team doctors watched over their VIP Quarterback very carefully, always investigating even the slightest indication of some physical malady. Plus, the 'Med Chip' embedded in his forearm never sounded alarms of any kind. To be sure, Quarterback Sean Callahan was in 'perfect health.'

And so, two weeks later, on a cold January morning, Mr. Callahan's package arrived.

He couldn't wait to open it. How long would he be on the right side of the grass? Basking in the sun on some faraway beach in the Caribbean; grandchildren at his knee, while he spun stories of his NFL football adventures.

Disappointed is a violent understatement of emotion as he read the cover letter of the prognosis report.

"How can this be? There must be some mistake!"

According to this report, there would be no Caribbean beaches or even grandchildren. In fact, there wouldn't even be another month to enjoy life.

Read on my friend!

UNITED GLOBAL LIFE AND CASUALTY

01/10/2043

Dear Mr. Callahan:

It is with sincere regret that we are writing you today to inform you of the prognosis for your report. After an intensive double review of your physical and associated lifestyle and ancestral questionnaires, we have determined that your demise will occur on the following date:

February 14th, 2044

Because this date is imminent, we strongly urge you to seek medical advice regarding your condition as, perhaps, health professionals may be able to prolong your longevity.

Additionally, while we are confident that our prognosis provides you with an accurate life expectancy, mistakes are sometimes made and it is important to note that, as is enumerated in our attached disclaimer documents; while our patented actuarial process has been clinically proven to have a high degree of accuracy (98.6%), it is not guaranteed to be one hundred percent precise.

Please review the detailed elements included in this report demonstrating the methods by which we arrived at your prognosis.

Again, please accept our sincere regret for our prognosis of your imminent demise. We want to thank you for your patronage of United Global Life and Casualty

Sincerely,

Madeline Swathmore

Madeline Swathmore
Vice President/Account Services.
P: 800-727-9800
E: M.Swathmore@UnitedGlobal.com

Sean Callahan was incredulous. The Oklahoma Oilers had just won their ninth AFC championship.

They were on to the Super Bowl on the very day he was scheduled to expire from this earth!

Digging deeper into the prognosis report, he discovered that he was a victim of a rare neurological disease named after Lewis Carroll's book, "The Adventures of Alice in Wonderland." The neurological disorder is called Alice in Wonderland Syndrome or AIWS.

The disorder is extremely rare, difficult to diagnose, and untreatable. *(I'm aware this condition may sound unbelievable to you Mr. or Ms.r reader, so I invite you to Google it. It's real.)* It is almost always fatal within one year. Some symptoms are migraines and a distorted view of one's own and others' appendages. Hallucinations are common. Hands and arms will appear to the victim as much larger than their actual size.

Sean Callahan was in denial. This could not be happening to him. Though secretly, he had had episodes of the very symptoms described in the report. Migraines, perceived distortions of body parts, etc. But these were temporary, mostly momentary events not to be paid serious attention.

He decided to keep all of this to himself. At least until after the Super Bowl. After all the physicals, attention, and wellness sessions with the Team's physicians, no one ever suggested he suffered from any serious physical ailments. Besides, United Global themselves put a disclaimer on their reports indicating that they aren't *always* accurate.

February 13th was a tough day for Sean. He generally didn't sleep well the night before the Super Bowl, but he would get absolutely none tonight.

And then, the big day came with all its pageantry and hoopla. Surprisingly, even with no sleep, Sean felt solid and vibrant. Maybe this was just all a bad dream.

Everything was going well. At halftime, the Oilers led 21-3. Super Star Sean Callahan threw three touchdown passes, and his oilers dominated the entire time.

The second half opened with yet another 38-yard TD pass to his favorite receiver. And then, things changed. Sean's right hand seemed to grow three times its normal size right before his eyes.

"What the Hell is this?"

He couldn't shake it. He bent over his Center Lineman with his perceived mutated right hand to receive the snap, and then, he collapsed right into the offensive line and dropped dead.

It seems United Global Life and Casualty had lived up to their 98.6% accuracy. The entire stadium erupted in wild convulsive disbelief. The greatest Quarterback of all time lay dead on the 18- yard line of Consumer Arena. Indeed, players were injured, sometimes seriously. But no one had ever *died* in the Super Bowl. Should the game still proceed? Be suspended?

Accordingly, *"The show must go on!"* (So, to speak) and the game continued. Even though Quarterback Callahan's lifeless body was carried off the field, the spectators could only guess just how badly he was injured. Nothing of his demise came over the loudspeaker, and the announcers in the booth only knew that he was seriously injured and had been taken into the medical tent and would likely not return to the game. No one had been informed of their Quarterback's demise, and the backup to Callahan played with fantastic skill.

Even so, the oilers never scored the rest of the game again, and the opposing Arizona Cougars fought their way back to win the LXXVII Super Bowl 28–21.

Still, even in his absence, Sean Callahan was once again elected MVP and, later that year, inducted posthumously to the National Football Hall of Fame.

He loved the game to death.

29

"Man's Best Friend"

You could say Doogie Kuchinek was a loner. His real first name was Donald, but everyone called him Doogie, though no one knew why, not even him. Anyway, at 62 years of age, he had no real friends, had never been married, and never even had a girlfriend. To be sure, there were acquaintances, like the carrier who brought the mail to the small acreage where he lived just outside of Dubois, Wyoming, population 1,113. Doogie himself had retired from the postal service a few years ago, so he would occasionally exchange small talk with the guy who came by with his packages and such.

But other than the infrequent interactions with people like that, Doogie had no social companions except for his faithful dog, Bella. Bella was a gorgeous, loving 2-year-old Golden Retriever who, as far as Doogie was concerned, was all the company he needed.

Bella would spend her days happily chasing squirrels and running and jumping around the trees and fields of the acreage while Doogie worked on restoring his classic 2022 Chevrolet Corvette Stingray.

One day, a family of Raccoons sets up shop on the outer edges of the acreage. Raccoons can be ill-tempered critters who don't enjoy the company of other animals, maybe, especially dogs.

Generally, Raccoons are nocturnal animals, but sometimes they venture out during the day searching for food. That's when Bella ran into trouble.

Still more of a puppy than a dog, Bella came upon one of the elder members of the family and, out of curiosity more than anything, she cautiously approached the prickly animal. Maybe he wanted to play? He didn't. The Racoon jumped at Bella and bit her directly behind her right leg, drawing blood.

That was enough. Bella turned and ran from the crazed coon, limping her way home to rest on the front porch of the house. From the garage, Doogie heard a murmured, dog-like whimpering and came out to see what was going on. There was Bella, splayed out on the wooden planks crying the way dogs do when they're scolded or hurt.

On closer inspection, Doogie noticed a nasty bite mark on her right leg. Doogie helped her into the house. There he dressed the bite wound and bandaged her.

"How'd this happen girl? Coyote? Skunk? What bit you?"

Of course, Bella couldn't answer, she just limped to her kennel and laid down. She'd stopped crying and Doogie figured she'd be alright by the next day.

Morning came. Bella still wasn't herself. She seemed listless. Doogie brought some dog food and water to her kennel, but she wasn't interested in either. He reached down to pet her on the nape of her neck. That seemed to comfort her as she pulled her head up and licked his face, affectionately.

"It's ok girl! You just rest today. We'll get you feeling better."

Doogie thought it strange that Bella seemed so lethargic. Something was wrong. He was inclined to just pull her up on his lap on the couch, but he had work to do. He ambled out to the garage and spent most of the morning working on the Corvette.

Around noon, he came back to the house to get a bite to eat and check on Bella. She hadn't moved from her kennel and never touched the food or water he'd brought to her earlier. He decided to just stay with her for a while, lifting her up and sitting her on his lap, and just stroking her back. She, in turn, would occasionally reach back and return the affection with laps of her tongue on his face.

Doogie wasn't sure what to do. This sure wasn't the Bella he knew. Could that bite mark have been that bad? Years ago, there was a Vet in Dubois, but he had long since left the town.

Day two wasn't any better. In fact, as Doogie got up out of bed walking over to check on her, poor Bella lay motionless and still had not touched her food or water. Upon seeing Doogie, she managed to get up out of her kennel, but she was staggering around and wasn't moving well.

Doogie wasn't sure what to do. The nearest Veterinarian was in Johnson Hole, almost a two-hour drive away. He loved his Bella and would gladly take the trip if he thought it was necessary. He decided to give it just one more day. If she wasn't better in the morning, he'd haul her in the pickup and head off to Johnson Hole.

Day three. Same thing. Motionless. The fresh food and water he placed in her kennel were untouched. Doogie reached in her kennel to help her out into the room, but Bella wasn't cooperating. Then Doogie realized the problem. Bella had died in the night. Eyes wide open with no spark of life. Drool had fallen from her canine jaw.

Doogie was crestfallen! A wave of unbearable grief came over him and chilled him to the bone. Overnight, while he slept, he had truly lost his best and only friend. He moved over to the sofa beside Bella's kennel, put his head in his hands, and began to sob like a parent losing their child.

It was hours before he was able to compose himself. He would have to go through this enormous anguish by himself. No companion to comfort him or share his grief and mourning. In time, he would bury her just a few yards from the house.

Weeks went by and the pain and misery of losing Bella had not subsided. It held Doogie emotionally hostage. He felt no better than the moment he discovered her lying dead in her kennel.

For Doogie, who had no friends or relatives to lean on, this was devastating. How long would he have to go on living in this emotional Hell? Get another dog? No! There was no pet who could replace his Bella.

Doogie had heard folks talking in town about the United Global Life and Casualty Prognosis Project. They could tell you how much longer you had to live and, for an additional fee, the probable cause of your demise. He decided he would sign up. At least he'd know how long he had to endure life on this planet.

And so, he made the appointment and drove the two hours to Johnson Hole for the testing process. He would receive his report by certified mail in approximately two weeks.

Surprisingly, in 5 short days, a FedEx truck brought a manila envelope that required a signature by the recipient!

"Sign here please!"

Unlike most individuals who had signed on to the United Global Project, Doogie wasn't all excited about it. He just wanted to know the score. But what he read in the cover letter brought him shock and dismay!

UNITED GLOBAL LIFE AND CASUALTY

November 14th, 2039

Mr. Donald Kuchinek
117 Rodeo Road
Dubois, Wyoming

Dear Mr. Kuchinek:

It is with sincere regret that after a thorough examination and review of your current condition we at United Global Life and Casualty have concluded that your expiration date will commence on:

.

November 30th, 2039

Please note, that because the date of your demise is imminent, we have expedited this report via overnight Federal Express.

While in the process of examination of your blood serum and hair follicles, our physicians have ascertained that you have, somehow, contracted the rabies virus. Therefore, we strongly urge you to contact a physician at your earliest opportunity as they may be able to extend your longevity.

We would like to remind you that, as is enumerated in our disclaimer documents; while our proprietary actuarial process has been clinically proven to have a high degree of accuracy (98.6%) it is not guaranteed to be one hundred percent precise.

Yours Truly,

Madeline Swathmore

Madeline Swathmore
Vice President/Account Services.
P: 800-727-9800
E: M.Swathmore@UnitedGlobal.com

Upon reading the letter, Doogie was beside himself.

"Damn! Of course! That's what was wrong with Bella!"

Right now, death didn't seem like such a good idea to Doogie. Especially dying with the horrific pain and suffering of rabies. He rushed out to his pick-up and headed straight for the Dubois Clinic.

He showed the doctor, the letter from United Global to which the doctor began asking questions about Doogie's symptoms. Even today, there is no cure for rabies and once there are symptoms, rabies is almost always 100% fatal. But symptoms of rabies can appear from a few days to more than a year after exposure. Bella had apparently contracted the virus from the raccoon bite and transmitted it to Doogie when she licked his face with her saliva.

"Ok Mr. Kuchinek, have you been bitten anywhere in the recent past?"

Doogie shook his head from side to side indicating he had not.

"Uh. No! But my dog unexpectantly died recently!"

"Ahh! Did your dog have difficulty swallowing, drooling, anything like that?"

"Well, yes! I guess so. She refused to eat or drink for days and when I found her dead she had drooled onto her kennel!"

Hearing that, the doctor looked at Doggie curiously and said:

"Alright! Have you had a fever, headache, muscle aches, loss of appetite, or nausea lately?"

"Nope! I feel ok! Nothing like that!"

"Alright, that's the good news. The bad news is, we're going to have to give you injections of rabies monoclonal antibodies several times over the next month."

Doogie was flabbergasted at the doctor's remarks.

"Will that cure me?"

"Hopefully. It's good you came to us when you did before you had symptoms. these injections are no picnic. They're going to be painful. And, we must start them right away today.

(Three-legged dog walks into a bar; says, 'I'm here to find the man who shot my paw!')

Doogie survived.

30

"Change of Heart, Change of Mind"

MARY ALICE CUNNINGHAM LOVED HER LIFE. Sixty-Three years old, married at 18 for forty-five joyous years to William (Bill) Cunningham. Mary Alices' life revolved around her husband. Though they never had any children, that was fine with them both. It allowed them the freedom to go where they wanted and do what they wanted when they wanted.

And they did. They traveled the world together; attended concerts and parties and sporting events, couples golf leagues, the works. Mary Alice lived to please Bill. For all of forty-five years whatever he wanted from her, she would devotedly provide. She was consumed with love for her life-long soul mate. It was the perfect marriage. Or so she thought.

One early Friday evening, Bill came home from work, kissed his wife, and sat down to the romantic candlelight dinner Mary Alice, by tradition, prepared for him to begin every weekend.

But this night there would be no romance. This night, Bill had a stern look on his face.

This was a little frightening to Mary Alice. Bill had a solemn look on his face she hadn't seen before:

"Is something wrong sweetie? You seem distant tonight. Rough day at work?"

Bill's face grew taut. This was serious:

"Mary, we have to talk. Something has happened in my life."

She walked towards him, attempting an embrace:

"Oh Baby! You can tell me anything. What is it? Are you ill? Did you lose your job? Please confide in me!"

Bill shunned away from her:

"It's nothing like that Mary. It's..."

Astonished at his pulling back, she submissively said:

"It's what?"

He couldn't play this game with her anymore. He blurted out the devastating words:

"I might as well get right to it. Mary Alice, I'm in love with another woman!"

She was losing patience. He was dragging this on much too long:

"Sure, you are Sweetheart. That's not funny, now please tell me what's wrong! What happened?"

One more time:

"That's what's wrong. I've fallen in love with another woman. I'm leaving you, Mary Alice.,"

Mary Alice was in complete and utter disbelief:

"Oh my God! That's not true! That's simply not true! Bill! What the hell's wrong with you tonight? You're not leaving me, and you don't love some other woman! Now. Let's just sit down and eat dinner before it gets cold. We'll go out for drinks later and you can tell me what really happened."

But Bill Cunningham's facial demeanor and voice timbre didn't change.

"I'm so sorry Mary, at this point, it's beyond my control. I'm in too deep. I packed some of my things last night while you were out. I'll be leaving here in a bit. I just wanted to do the right thing and tell you in person."

With that Mary Alice began to scream, shaking her arms in the air convulsively.

"No! No! No! Stop this now! Right now! Bill, this isn't funny! Please, dear God no!

Oddly, Bill seemed dispassionate. Now silent, he quietly got up from the table, walked briskly to the door, out to his car, and drove away to some unknown destination.

Inside, Mary Alice was disconsolate. Surely this was just a surreal nightmare. Like what happened really didn't happen. Forty-Five Years in a beautiful marriage. Childhood Sweethearts and one day, forty-five years later, her life partner and soul mate comes home with *this*.

A stark chill came over Mary Alice. Sobbing, bawling in disbelief as she leaned over the still burning candles on the dining room table. Bill Cunningham was her life. She willingly lived solely in his shadow. And now, in a moment's time, life as she knew it was over. This was all real.

He's gone! Within minutes she began to contemplate suicide; went into the kitchen to find a big, sturdy knife. Immediately, she found the instrument she needed but was unable to execute her impulsive intention.

"What if he just had a momentary lapse? Maybe he'll come back tonight. Surely, he'll come back. I need to be here for him when he arrives."

Mary Alice sat down in the living room, still crying uncontrollably; waiting for her Bill to come back home. Minutes passing seemed like hours, hours like days. On into the wee hours of the morning, Mary Alice sat staring at the front door. But it was not to be. Her Bill had literally and permanently driven out and away from his marriage.

Somewhere in the night, a fretful sleep overcame her as she slumped down into the same sofa chair that accommodated her wet, wailing eyes. She awoke in the morning around 7 a.m., still alone in the now eerily silent home.

Nearly a week of constant anguish went by. In the following days, Bill Cunningham would keep watch on her movements. When Mary Alice was away from the house, he crept in and cleaned out his belongings.

Upon discovering this, she began to accept that Bill was gone for good. There are stories of individuals who, having broken an extremity, have driven themselves to the hospital for treatment. We wonder: "How were they able to do that?" Mary Alice Cunningham drove around aimlessly for weeks with a broken heart. How did she do that? There are no 'Broken Heart Hospitals.' You just deal with it. No one can see it. It can't be treated except by time. She could barely cope except for continuous doses of Xanax in the medicine cabinet prescribed by her physician some months ago for anxiety. But 'anxiety' was a severe understatement. She'd kill for just a *little* anxiety.

"Where could he be? Who is he with? Who is this woman? When did he meet her? How did he fall in love? Our life was so good and beautiful. How could he do this to me? I'll find him!

I'll find him and make love to him! Then he'll remember. He'll realize he's not in love with someone else."

But this was all wishful thinking. Over the course of a month gone by, Mary Alice had lost more than twenty pounds. At least money wasn't an issue. She and Bill had accounts worth more than a million dollars plus. He enjoyed an extremely good income as a partner in his Law Firm and had the decency to leave their mutual savings to her.

Mary Alice used some of those funds to hire a private investigator to find out just what was going on and discover who this woman could possibly be.

The P.I. did his job well. A few days after he signed on, he brought back pictures of the enthralled couple together. Apparently, the woman was Bill's para-legal, Carole Ann Baldoff; barely Thirty years old and drop-dead gorgeous.

The P.I. offered a warning to Mary Alice, as he had some rather lascivious pics of the two of them in bed together at her apartment. Perhaps she would prefer not to see them. Upon her insistence, he handed them over.

That was enough. After months of wishing and hoping and waiting and wailing, Mary Alice decided she would have one last cry. In her mind, suicide was no longer a real option. But she really did not want to live. Everything she held dear in life; everything that brought her joy was gone forever.

Like almost everyone, she had heard about the United Casualty Prognosis Project. When they were together, she and Bill would sometimes ponder about it, each deciding that they'd rather not know the unthinkable when they would one day leave the other alone on the planet.

But times changed. Things were different now. Mary Alice would submit to the testing that would divulge the moment of her demise. She hoped it would be soon. She no longer had anything meaningful in her life. Plus, she had lost so much weight, she had withered away to an 89lb. stick. Surely, the stress was killing her. And so, she proceeded.

It didn't take long. In the United Global tradition, Mary Alice Cunningham acquired her 'Death Day Prognosis' in just fifteen days.

UNITED GLOBAL LIFE AND CASUALTY

September 29th, 2039

Mrs. Mary Alice Cunningham
1322 Solidra Road,
Elk Grove, Illinois

Dear Mrs. Cunningham:

It is with sincere regret that after a thorough examination and thrice review of your current physical condition. we at United Global Life and Casualty have concluded that your expiration date will commence on:

December 5th, 2039

As you did not subscribe to our "probable cause" option, we are unable to provide you with the exact origin of your malady. However, we strongly recommend you consult with your physician at your earliest opportunity, as there may be a medical solution that will extend your longevity.

In addition, we would like to remind you that, as is enumerated in the attached disclaimer documents; while our proprietary actuarial process has been clinically proven to have a high degree of accuracy (98.6%) it is not guaranteed to be one hundred percent precise.

Sincerely,
Madeline Swathmore

Madeline Swathmore
Vice President/Account Services.
P: 800-727-9800
E: M.Swathmore@UnitedGlobal.com

While the Prognosis Report would cause severe anxiety for most, Mary Alice was somewhat relieved to see she had about two-and-one-half miserable months left to reside on this side of the grass.

"It's probably a heart attack or some such thing. Because they just can't say the truth:

'She died of a broken heart'"

She would not visit her physician or any doctor or health professional for that matter. For all intents and purposes, Mary Alice Cunningham's life was over the day her Bill drove away into the arms of that 'other' woman.

She wasn't a particularly religious woman, but soon after her husband abandoned her, Mary Alice began going to church. In some moments, she garnered a kind of comfort in her faith. For the most part, she shunned parish activities, but one day after morning Sunday service, she decided to attend the afternoon brunch in the Church basement.

A couple of dozen parishioners had shown up, congregating amongst themselves at the tables. As Mary Alice had not socialized with anyone, she relegated herself to the one empty table where she would sit alone hoping someone, anyone, would find a seat beside her.

"Ask and you shall receive!"

Within moments, the most handsome singular specimen of a man came up to her and asked the proverbial:

"Pardon me ma'am, is this seat taken?"

Visibly taken aback, Mary Alice half stuttered: *"Why no sir, there's no one sitting here"*

"Perfect! Would you mind if I sat with you? I'm new to this congregation, I don't know anyone."

Apparently, there is a God:

"That will be fine sir. Please sit down!"

As it turned out, the stranger was a great conversationalist. His name was "Bill" (Go figure) sixty-seven years old, widowed, and obviously enjoyed the time spent with this now available, Mary Alice Cunningham.

One thing led to another, and soon, "Bill" asked if they might see each other again soon. Mary Alice was awestruck. They happily exchanged contact information and after a time, Bill Costas walked Mary Alice Cunningham to her car. It was late October 2039.

Mary Alice slept well that night. Finally, there was some light in her life, albeit just a small flicker.

In the next three weeks, she and Bill connected several times. At some point, they decided they would spend Thanksgiving together, just the two of them. She would prepare a small turkey with of course all the trimmings, and he would bring a bottle of an extra special Pinot Noir.

Mary Alice just picked at her food, but Thanksgiving Day (and evening) was delicious in every sense of the word. Mary Alice made an incomparable meal for them and as always, the two of them enjoyed each other's company immensely. Finally, the evening ended with passionate lovemaking. Bill turned out to be a crafted lover and Mary Alice responded with complete abandon.

Of course, Bill stayed the night and morning arrived with a satisfaction neither had known for some time. He would stay the weekend.

When he left Monday morning, they kissed goodbye, and Mary Alice had a glow about her that was almost visible. For the first time in forever, she was alive! Really alive! She had never realized how truly shallow her forty-five-year betrothal really was. The new Bill was all the man she would ever need. To complete her euphoria Bill called later that day to express that he felt he was falling in love with her. It was "Mary Alice in Wonderland" as she responded in kind.

Caught up in the rapture, Mary Alice completely forgot all about the United Global Life and Casualty prognosis. If they were right, Mary Alice Cunningham was going to die in just nine days. The med-chip in her arm wasn't alerting her to any problems, so maybe they were wrong.

Now, aware of the imminent peril of her probable upcoming demise, she frantically drove herself to the nearest Emergency Room. There she waited for two hours before she was attended to. Indeed, Mary Alice was a very sick woman.

The Health Professionals diagnosed her with a condition known as Anorexia Nervosa, a malady that ended the life of a popular vocalist in the 1970s named Karen Carpenter. Put into layman's terms, it is an eating disorder, characterized by abnormally low body weight, and a distorted perception of how she really looked. Mary Alice was five foot three inches tall and weighed just 80 pounds. The 'Med-Chip' embedded in her forearm was unlikely to have sensed the condition.

For most with this disorder, the prognosis is organ failure or myocardial infarction (heart attack). And that is exactly what happened to Mary Alice Cunningham, right there on the floor of the ER.

Luckily, the cardiac event happened with Health Professionals all around and they were able to revive her. However, treatment for Anorexia Nervosa is simply getting the patient back to a healthy height/weight proportionate weight.

Too little, too late. Mary Alice Cunningham succumbed to her condition, just as United Global had predicted, on December 5th, 2039. A grief-stricken William Costas would be the only person attending the funeral. Ex-husband Bill would have shown, but he had to rearrange his sock drawer.

31

"Non-Refundable"

MICHAEL SANDUSKY LIVED IN OMAHA, Nebraska. Home of the headquarters of United Global Life and Casualty. For months he had been contemplating subscribing to the United Global Prognosis Project, he just wasn't sure if he really wanted to know the day or probable cause of his earthly termination. To add to his ambivalence, Michael was a very religious individual.

"Would it be right to enquire about your Death Day? Was it some kind of sin?"

He just didn't know. He decided to call his local parish priest, Father Robert. Surely, he would know the answer to this conundrum.

"Hello! Father Robert here! How can I help you?"

"Father, this is Michael Sandusky! Do you have a minute!"

"Sure, Mike! What's up?"

"Well, I'm sure you've heard about that United Global Life Prognosis Project, haven't you?"

"You mean that thing where they tell you when you're going to die?"

"Yes! I've considered subscribing to the process but, I wondered if you thought that it might be a sin against God."

"Hmm...that's a tough one, Mike! But if it is, from my observation, there's a whole lot of people right here in town who are heading for Hell right now. The bigger question is, do you really want to know?"

"That's just it! I've been going back and forth on this ever since it came out!"

"Well, Mike, I can't make that decision for you, but personally, I don't think doing it is any Kind of a sin."

"Well, that, at least helps a lot, Father. Thanks so much! I'll let you know what I decide."

"Okie Doke Mike. Good luck!"

Now, with the conversation over, they hung up simultaneously, and Michael continued his contemplation. So much to consider. Eventually, his intense curiosity got the better of him and he decided, he'd do it! He called down to the Omaha United Global agent and booked the lab appointment.

The whole process only took about an hour. First, came the non-refundable contractual agreement. With the optional 'probable cause' it was $4200 digital cash. Then, blood work, DNA swab, Urinalysis, you know the drill.

All the info was immediately assessed by the lab next door and the report was sent to the Actuary Department at United Global.

Michael went home, still unsure if he had done the right thing, but it was over now, 'water under the bridge' so to speak. He sat down in the living room and turned the six o'clock news on the Hologram Vision Screen.

"What is this?"

Sure enough, right there in front of him on the National News Channel, was a crowd of three or four hundred protestors parading in front of the United Global Omaha headquarters, shouting, and marching with big signs that read:

"Mark 13:33! You do not know when the time will come!" And

"United Global Blasphemous!"

"Thessalonians 5.2, The Day of the Lord will come like a thief in the night!"

The video hologram then cut to the Vatican where the Pope, standing on the balcony of Saint Peters Basilica, proclaimed the very same. United Global Life and Casualty was guilty of a sacrilegious and ungodly practice, offensive to our God Almighty and all the saints and angels in the heavens and on earth!

Michael was beside himself. Less than an hour ago, he had committed himself to the very act that even the Pope had decreed was an egregious sin. The United Global Agent Office was surely closed for the day, but first thing tomorrow he would call and cancel his submission.

"Hello, United Global Life and Casualty! Agent Thomas Carlson speaking."

"Tom! This is Michael Sandusky.   I was in yesterday for my Prognosis processing."

Tom Carlson looked up from his embedded speaker arm. "What could he possibly want?"

"Yes! Hello Mr. Sandusky! How can I help you?"

With the most assertive and emphatic voice he could muster, Michael said:

"Well, Tom, I want to cancel my submission. I've changed my mind."

"Wow! That's discouraging Mr. Sandusky! What seems to be the problem?"

"Tom! I saw the protests on the news yesterday and then the Pope came out and disparaged your whole program! I'm a good Catholic. I just can't tolerate this thing. I need to cancel and have you refund my money."

"I'm so sorry Mr. Sandusky. As you are probably aware, we've already sent your lab results to headquarters. They're working on your report as we speak. It's too late! And, as you know our agreement states your payment is non-refundable."

Michael anticipated this response. He was ready for it. He decided to go to 'Plan B' the nuclear option:

"Well, I'm sorry to hear that Tom, but as you are surely aware, Nebraska State Law legally allows cancellation of any contract within three days of signing."

"Uh...I'm not aware of that statute Mr. Sandusky, but I've never encountered this situation before. No one has ever asked for their money back. As I said the processing of your report has already begun.

"Well, why don't you check with your supervisor, and we'll just see how that works for you. I said, I want to cancel the contract, and I want my money back. If you don't acquiesce, the nnext person you'll hear from is my attorney!"

As it turned out, United Global could have fought Mike Sandusky for his refund, and likely prevailed, as the services he paid for had begun. But, with all the current bad publicity, protests, and news, not to mention the Pope's condemnations. Management decided it was in their best interest to forego the battle and refund Mr. Sandusky's funds.

However, United's Actuarial Department was not notified of the cancellation and proceeded to work on Michael Sandusky's prognosis and probable cause of death.

A month passed. Surprisingly, Mr. Sandusky received a letter in the mail with the return address: United Global Life and Casualty.

"Aren't they finished with me? Why don't they just leave me alone?" Casually, he opened the letter.

UNITED GLOBAL LIFE AND CASUALTY

October 26th, 2040

Mr. Michael Sandusky
17120 Cedar Plaza.
Omaha, Ne. 68130

Dear Mr. Sandusky:

United Global Life and Casualty has received the cancellation notice of your Prognosis Project report. It is with sincere regret that you decided to forego our services.

However, despite the successful cancellation of your report, the process of determining the day and probable cause of your demise had already proceeded and was completed in our underwriting Actuarial Department.

Though we are now prohibited from providing you with the date and probable cause, we feel compelled to caution you to be aware that you are in imminent danger of expiring in the very near future and would strongly advise you to consult your physician or health professional at your earliest opportunity.

We wish to thank you for your consideration of our services and we wish you the very best of health in the future!

Sincerely,

Madeline Swathmore

Madeline Swathmore
Vice President/Account Services.
P: 800-727-9800
E: M.Swathmore@UnitedGlobal.com

Upon reading the communication from the Insurance company, Michael Sandusky almost lost his breath.

In a panic, he ran to his vehicle, plugged in the coordinates to the nearest hospital Emergency Room, started the engine, and flew off to his destination with anticipatory anxiety and terror.

As the vehicle pulled up to the hospital ER. The attendants came out to see a man slumped over the manual steering wheel, motionless. Michael Sandusky had died on the way to the hospital of cardiac arrest.

Did Mr. Sandusky go to Heaven or a place somewhat warmer? We don't really know. On the one hand, he paid for the program, and on the other, he canceled out of fear of sin. If we get a chance, we'll ask the Pope. Amen.

"Guilty Conscience"

THE NATIONALLY TELEVISED PROTESTS outside United Global HQ did a lot of detriment to their 'Prognosis Project.' The protests alone were bad enough, but when the Pope stuck his nose in the fray calling it 'Sacrilegious,' There were calls for a boycott of the company on every church pulpit in America.

Business dropped 18% in just the following week. Still, here in 2045, science has much-upended religion, and religious church membership has fallen considerably in the previous decades.

However, though fewer now, many atheistic, agnostic, and less impassioned religious souls were still paying good money to see how much time they have left to enjoy their life here on earth. The volume of Prognosis applications was still quite voluminous, still, the Underwriting and Actuarial department personnel were somewhat relieved at the diminished workload.

But now, there was a cog in the wheel. In the aftermath of the protests etc., certain individual United Global employees whom, shall we say, were more 'Fervently Religious', began to question their occupations.

"Was compiling these reports really a sin against God and Humanity? Would they be spending eternity in Hell for committing to this ominous livelihood?"

Hard to say but based on the Pope's utterings and the local parish pastor's sermons on Sundays, maybe it was time for a career change. Hook up with another Insurance company...

OR

Maybe they could exact a way to end this irreverent United Global Venture.

Surely you remember Madeline Swathmore. She's Vice President of Account Services and the one who signed most of the letters to participants in the 'Prognosis Project'.

Well, turns out, Madeline went to church every Sunday religiously. (Pun intended). One day, while looking for an empty table at lunch in the HQ Cafeteria, she happened upon Brett Lindstrom, Chief Actuary on the Prognosis Project.

"Hi, Brett! Mind if I sit here?"

"Not at all, Madeline, it's good to see you!"

"How're you doing these days Brett?"

Waving his hands straight in the air and moving his head side to side he said:

"Well, I won't lie, Madeline, it's been rough lately! Protestors outside the building every day going to and from work. Problem is, I'm not sure I disagree with their cause."

"That's interesting Brett. I'm beginning to have misgivings myself. After the Pope came out with his disparaging comments about the project, I'm not sure I can do this much longer."

A disgusted look came over him:

'You know, I wish they'd just close it down. This thing has gotten out of hand. We're getting bad press all over the place and I'm starting to worry about my safety! Those protestors outside are beginning to get unruly!"

'I'm so glad you said that, Brett! I've been thinking long and hard about this. Maybe there IS something we can do!"

Quizzically:

"Uh, like what?"

"Well, I have an idea. Perhaps you and I can work on it together. It may end this entire fiasco and the company can go back to selling insurance like we originally intended."

With that, Madeline began to explain the plan she had been devising for weeks now. Brett Lindstrom was just the partner she needed to execute. To be sure, it was probably illegal, surely unethical, and maybe even immoral, but combined with the public influence of the religious protestors it could surely put an end to United Global's blasphemous Prognosis Project.

Together, what they would do, is send out revised, grossly inaccurate communications to Prognosis Project recipients, contrary to what the rank-and-file Actuaries had prognosticated. Those reports that were determined to project a long, fruitful existence on this planet, would be revised to indicate that their demise was imminent. Those whose demise *was* imminent would be informed that they would continue to live for decades.

Chaos would ensue. The 98.6% accuracy of the United Global Prognosis Project would be skewed downward as individuals who were told they could look forward to many long, nourishing years, would unexpectedly be dropping dead. And those who were warned of imminent demise would just sail through the date of their supposed ending.

Brett was at first reluctant to be a part of Madeline's plan. But, after some contemplation, he decided it would be the one thing that would end this madness. He decided he would join her in the endeavor.

And so, whatever report his Actuarial team brought to him, he would reverse the report and hand it off to Madeline Swarthmore.

She, in turn, would send out a communication that was intentionally inaccurate and bogus.

Soon, individuals who considered they had a long life ahead of them were dying prematurely and those who were informed they would leave this world in the very near future were living long past the day of their scheduled demise.

The disclaimer on all reports indemnified United Global life and Casualty but as this continued, the public began to distrust the reports sent out by the company. Applications for the report began to drop even more precipitously. Now, applications were less than 50% year over year.

A deep investigation into just what was happening was ensured. How could a system that was inviolately dependable, suddenly be so completely inaccurate?

It wasn't long before United Global execs. discovered just what was going on. The sabotage plan devised by Madeline Swathmore and partnered with Brett Lindstrom was exposed and revealed.

This was, of course, criminal. But what could United Global management do? Could they announce the discovery? Prosecute the perpetrators? That would bring down the house!

The media would excoriate and vilify the entire operation. People would demand refunds en masse. It would be economic suicide for the entire company. How could this be explained to the public?

In the end, they would quietly shut down the entire Prognosis Project. Madeline Swathmore and Brett Lindstrom would both be terminated with a healthy severance package, provided they do not disclose their actions in any form to the public or the media.

And so, the United Global Life and Casualty Prognosis Project ironically died the untimely death they reported to a multitude of curious citizens.

The evening of the public announcement of the end of the project, Madeline and Brett had dinner at an upscale restaurant. They toasted to a happy ending to an evil, blasphemous, program, promulgated by a 'money hungry' insurance company.

Their severance packages were considerable. Both would have financial security for the rest of their lives. Meanwhile, neither would miss church on Sunday.

"Believe it, or not!"

WELL, THIS IS A CONUNDRUM. We finally succumbed to our own curiosity and decided we wanted to know the day, month, and year of our demise.

The problem is that we're not sure if we participated in the Prognosis Project before or after the Madeline Swathmore and Brett Lindstrom fiasco.

The letter I received informed me that I could look forward to 42 more glorious years on this wonderful sphere that rotates around the sun. Some of the others helping in this Chronicle weren't so fortunate. But was this a reversal communication, orchestrated by Madeline and Brett? Or was this a legitimate prognosis?

I feel pretty good, and my 'Med Chip' isn't sending me any alarms. But...

Anyway, when you get here, on or about 2035, if you're curious to know your 'Death Day' our suggestion is to do it at your earliest convenience. After 2045 it's a crapshoot whether you're going to get accurate information.

Oh! And Kerry Richmond? He never did process his own prognosis. He's living somewhere on an Indonesian Island, pampered by beautiful native women in the tradition of Marlon Brando.

Meanwhile, I may, or may not still be around when you get here. I guess it all depends on whether my Prognosis report was delivered before or after the Swathmore/Lindstrom interference.

Ahh Well! See you when you get here. I hope.

Acknowledgements

This book could not have been written without the expert editing skills of Hannah VanVels Ausbury. Hannah turned what was a very mediocre transcript into something readable.

I would recommend her to any aspiring author who needs their writings "Cleaned up"

She can be found on Reedsy.com in the editors catalog.

I would also like to recognize my friend and associate Randy Thompson for his valuable contributions to some of the contents in the book.

Contact information:

Ted Pysh
P: 402-578-7742
E: Weaverofwishes@yahoo.com

Other books by Theodore Pysh:

"The Immorals" (Amazon.com)
"Make me a Millionaire!" (Amazon.com)

Printed in Great Britain
by Amazon

32733682R00158